I0628523

THE WAR WITH
THE BELATRIN

The alien Belatrin are the "Other." They look like us, they organize their society like ours, yet even the slightest contact with them leads humans to madness. Here are seven encounters from a war in space that leads to a species-changing moment of synthesis and transformation, including the classic, award-winning novella, "The Five Biographies of General Gerrhan." First-rate space opera in the grand style!

Borgo Press Books by DON WEBB

*Do the Weird Crime, Serve the Weird Time: Tales of
    the Bizarre*
A Velvet of Vampyres: Tales of Horror
The War with the Belatrin: Science Fiction Stories
Webb's Weird Wild West: Western Tales of Horror

THE WAR WITH THE BELATRIN

SCIENCE FICTION STORIES

DON WEBB

THE BORGO PRESS

MMXII

THE WAR WITH THE BELATRIN

Copyright © 1992, 1997, 1998, 2011, 2012 by Don Webb

FIRST EDITION

Published by Wildside Press LLC

www.wildsidebooks.com

DEDICATION

For Harlan Ellison,

For everything—

But today for buying "Ching Witch"

CONTENTS

ACKNOWLEDGMENTS

"The Five Biographies of General Gerrhan" was first published in *Science Fiction Age*, Jan. 1997, and also in *To the Stars—and Beyond: The Second Borgo Press Book of Science Fiction Stories*, edited by Robert Reginald, Borgo Press, 2011. Copyright © 1997, 2011, 2012 by Don Webb.

"The Coming of the Spear" was first published in *Amazing Stories*, December 1992. Copyright © 1992, 2012 by Don Webb.

"Tamarii Notebook" was first published in *More Amazing Stories*, Tor Books, 1998. Copyright © 1998, 2012 by Don Webb.

"Talking to the Enemy" is published here for the first time. Copyright © 2012 by Don Webb.

"The Fleeing" is published here for the first time. Copyright © 2012 by Don Webb.

"A Tale from the War" was first published in *Science Fiction Age*, Vol. 1, No. 1, 1992. Copyright © 1992, 2012 by Don Webb.

"Mars 1, Burroughs 2" is published here for the first time. Copyright © 2012 by Don Webb.

THE FIVE BIOGRAPHIES OF GENERAL GERRHAN

I am Thomas Dam-Seuh Lasser.

I have written five biographies of General Helen Lyndon Gerrhan, who died in my bed shortly after the battle of Lister IV in the early decades of the Belatrin War. Most of my biographies have been suppressed, as have my earlier fiction, because of the effect the books were perceived to have on Terran and Siirian morale. However, the recent thawing up of writing gives me a chance to tell of the books' creation, and I do so, not out of bitterness for my long imprisonment, nor out of chance to renew my craft as writer, but out of the love for those scholars who will come along after me and put this brief essay in my collected works. The books of the past were a great help to me during the century of my imprisonment. The past is all prisoners have; there is no present beyond that first day which sets the pattern of their imprisonment, and there is no future since the future belongs to a god called Hope, who is forbidden to prisoners.

The first thing I want to say is that I did not know General Helen Lyndon. I will tell you what I experienced with her, but I have remembered (that is to say recreated) that incident so many times, I would put no more faith in its details than I would in any of my other fictions.

The War was new then. No one had seen one of the black Belatrin cruisers and lived to tell the tale before Helen. The Seventeenth Division of the Allied Force had been detached to the Lister system merely to observe the Belatrin. All of our encounters had ended in total annihilation of our forces, so the Seventeenth was merely to gather data and run away. There had been twenty-five dreadnoughts in the fleet; most had been destroyed by the Mind-Bomb. Three tried to take on a single Belatrin cruiser, and were vaporized. General Gerrhan's ship *The Pegasus* tried to warp away, but a streamer of the weapon we later came to call the *colours* touched the ship. Most of the crew died in transit. General Gerrhan and two of her aides survived. We didn't know at that time that willpower was the key to holding off the effect of the *colours*.

The three were Allied heroes. Everywhere they went, they were lionized. So they wanted to go somewhere—some backwater oniell colony or commercially pointless planet. You can't get any more commercially pointless than Angkor III.

In those days I lived on the government dole. The social engineers had tried to attract artist and writer types to the planet by establishing a good entitlements program. Writers will do anything rather than work for an honest wage. Except writing, of course, the real bane of our existence. I made love to exotic offworlders who looked like they had money.

I met her at Mary Denning's *King Suravarman's Dive*. It was full of local culture, exciting Angkorese music, flame sculpture, and our lovely cuisine. In short it was a tourist hell-hole.

She looked rich. Real rich. She had bright pink eyes like a rabbit, some lovely Maori tattoos, and her teeth were chrome. She looked like she was mean, and that she wanted someone to be mean to her. Her hair was long and purple, and it was the only thing she was wearing.

She was exactly my type. If I had been any poorer, any offworlder would have been exactly my type. She told me her name was Zohra Sibawaih. I told her my real name, and that my sister's name was Zohra (which is true).

I bought her a drink, she complimented me on my first book, *Stealing My Rules*. I knew then she had some very expensive data link. She hadn't even looked blankly to access the knowledge. But we both knew what the evening was about.

We went back to her hotel. We ordered some Noroolian spice tea. When our outlines got a little blurry we made love. A little roughly, which was when I figured she was military. Just before the telepathic rush came on, the *colours* hit.

She suddenly went into extra sharp focus. She looked like she was trying to scream.

Then the telepathic effect from the tea started. It

wasn't the rush of sex that you take the tea for. It wasn't even thoughts. When the telepathic rush hit me, I was paralyzed.

It was a series of geometric shapes and colors, that hurt you and hurt you, and made you feel like your brain was bleeding. It was simple shapes at first, just a little too big to fit in your mind, and it was colors that you knew. Then it was colors not of this universe, not sane colors, but colors with a meaning all their own. And shapes that shouldn't work out. And the smell of hot metals and of sex and of flowers that bloom in some pandemonium, and the shapes start tearing your mind to pieces. Then frenzied strains of an inhuman music, which decades later I can still remember. When I think about it, I can almost see shadowy satyrs and bacchanals dancing and whirling insanely through seething abysses of clouds and smoke and lightning. I could feel the *colours* sucking at her bone marrow, boiling her blood, shorting out her nervous system. There were pains and pleasures beyond endurance, and other moods and feelings there are no human words for—for humans weren't meant to feel them.

How long did this last? A couple of minutes objectively, thousands of years subjectively.

The *colours* stopped. I saw that a mere handful of bluish dust lay upon the bed, next to me. Then I fainted. I got up late in the night, and I went home. I thought of calling the police, but what would I say: "My one-night stand disintegrated?"

Allied Security sent a flyer to pick me up that afternoon. They're not real gentle, AS, they tore off the top of my house, and picked me up with a scoop. They flew me off to their headquarters.

A Free Machine interrogated me.

No, I did not know she was a general.

No, I had not met her before.

No, I did not cause the disintegration.

No, I did not know that something similar had happened to her aides.

No, I was not a spy.

They used a variety of mind probes on me. They weren't as advanced with those things then as they are now. Parts of my life were sucked away for good.

Then they took me to see the captain, a Siirian named U'ssmahzzrizzssuibz. It was molting, and tiny bits of its red carapace fell away during the interview.

"You know," U'ssmahzzrizzssuibz said, "you are in big trouble."

"How am I in trouble? I've done nothing."

"You were present at the death of someone the Allies want to make into a hero. You make that death tawdry."

"I know nothing about this woman. Let me go. I don't know anything about this woman. All I want to do is go back to writing."

"We can't let you do that. I have your profile." U'ssmahzzrizzssuibz tapped a small silver disk with his right claw. "Oh, I'm not interested in your petty larceny. It is the opinion of the Free Machine that interrogated you that having gone through such a traumatic experience as the *colours*, you cannot not begin to write about them."

That was true I had already begun (in my mind) to try to describe their ecstasy and terror.

"So," he said, "we can do one of two things. One, we can lock you up and deprive you of an audience while we are at war. Two, we censor your writings. Now I don't like socio-engineers, because I don't like being told what to do by humans. I have my own idea. We let you write about the general and about her death. But you write it as an heroic biography with a beautiful ending in her lover's arms."

"But I don't know anything about her. I don't follow the war effort, I find it too depressing."

"We can give you her life, at least as much of her life as the propaganda department thinks the Allies should know."

"I've never written nonfiction."

"Haven't you been paying attention? This will be fiction."

* * * * * * *

The book was *Helen: Why We Fight*. I did not come up with the title.

The first thing I had to change was my birth. Helen had been born and raised on Earth with an hereditary tie to the space army. So I changed my life. We had met at the Space Academy at Katmandu. She was a better than average student, and I was studying the Vajra paradigm of Tibet. I wanted to be bonded, but she had said that her career came first. Civilized space had given so much to her that she felt it was her duty to protect it. She had a near accident on Venus during a training flight. She graduated with honors.

I traced her rise through the ranks, her brilliant tactics during the Human-Siirian war. Her brief tour in the Exploration Service, which found three suitable worlds for human colonization.

She was going to retire and join me in a paradisical artists colony on Angkor III. Then she was caught in the surprise Belatrin attack on the Lister system. Valiantly she fought amidst blazing lasers and the insidious reality-warping devices of the Belatrin.

Finally having taken down one of their cruisers, she flew the crippled *Pegasus* home.

There I met her with flowers and wine and candlelight reciting my verses, when suddenly a strange fate pulled her from me.

It was a short book immediately made into all kinds of other media.

It sold on every planet, every ship, every asteroid, every oniell, and every Dyson sphere in the Alliance.

I had money, something my experimental writing had never brought me.

I got a Free Machine as an agent, and its first recommendation was write the book again in a longer version.

* * * * * *

The first book had been very hard to write. I am not a narrative-driven writer. I am language-driven. This means sound and philology turn me on, and money is something that other writers get. I figured the good stories, the ones that truly work the human psyche, have already been told as myths, so why should I contaminate the myth-sphere?

I know at one time people thought there would cease to be writers as new technologies bloomed, but as long as human brains have a left hemisphere, there will a place for the words-in-a-row guys.

The second book was called *HLG: Her Life and My Love.*

I am a fairly good parodist. An even century before the True Space Age, there has been a market for the space adventure novel. I don't know how many scholarly studies have been done showing how the early space adventure novel actually shaped both the myth and practice of space exploration. Anyway, I bought hundreds of these books, and read nothing but them.

Now at that time, you must remember, no one had *seen* Belatrin. The popular imagination considered them to be more or less physical beings, so with the blessing of the propaganda office, I gave Helen a sword and blaster, and had her lead an assault on the Belatrin ship itself. She told me the story on our wedding night. Oh yes, in the second book we were married under the stars of Angkor III.

We spent our few hours of wedded bliss with her rendition of the horrors of battle and her hope that, despite whatever fiendish obstacles the Belatrin had, the Allies would emerge victorious, strong and without the scars of the Human-Siirian war. We spent our honeymoon in the Hotel Splendide, using our meager money to buy the penthouse suite.

Of course, as an Allied general Helen would have been able to buy the hotel without blinking, but "meager money" is more becoming to a heroine.

I was making enough money from the first book to rent the penthouse suite fairly often, and I had enough of a reputation as a casualty of romance that I could have my pick of good-looking off-world women.

I dedicated the book to my younger sister, Zohra Kitab Lasser.

You may remember the passage where Helen takes on the Belatrin captain:

"It sprawled before me on its barbaric throne, this twelve-armed horror that had given the command that had melted the minds of the folk of Lister IV. Its baleful red eyes radiated a hatred of all that was good or sane in the cosmos. I needed to return to the *Pegasus*, but I wanted this moment to try and spill the ichor of this other leader.

"It heaved itself off its throne. Two of its pale purple tentacles held the tiny but powerful blasters that I had seen the crewmen use. It slithered toward me much faster than I had imagined such a boneless mass could move. I plunged forward swinging my sword. I would at least wound it, that was all that mattered.

"I never felt as great a pleasure as when my sword cut though the first throbbing tentacle."

When we really found out what the Belatrin were, during the False Peace Talks, the book was banned.

But the popular image of the Belatrin as a kind of phallic purple octopus entered the human collective unconsciousness through me.

I'll be honest. I had written the book way over the top. I didn't want it to do well. I was growing uncomfortable with the knowledge that what I would be known for was a cheap night's entertainment, and I even felt guilty because I was robbing so much from what had been a nice, but haunted, woman.

It was about then that I commissioned a portrait of Helen.

The book set records for sales that still stand today, a hundred years later. It was translated into languages and dialects of human and Siirian tongues that hadn't had new writing in decades. There wasn't a hut on Bemi III, or igloo on Earth, that lacked a copy. I had a library built on Angkor III that housed nothing but various copies of the book, and reproductions and adaptations in all existing media.

It was a big building.

The war was going very badly.

Zohra joined the army. She died in the battle of the Coal Sack Nebula.

My parents never spoke to me again.

* * * * * * *

I traveled as much as I could, the war stopping most planetary travel.

I swam in the seas of Earth, visited the ruins of New Mars, saw the lava sculpture festival on W'ssaterzzss, tasted the wines of Garcian II.

My earlier work had been reissued. It was dutifully bought by a patriotic publication, who was not in the habit of buying experimental prose. Small efforts of mine—poems written in my teens—a couple of songs I wrote—a sketch I had once made of a Siirian couple fornicating—were gathered and published.

Money came in and I tasted all the pleasures of the galaxy.

Oddly enough, I missed writing. I tried my hand at a few short stories, which were snapped up. I tried to squash a rumor that I was working on a third book about Helen.

There was a Belatrin attack on an oneill I was staying at. Because of who I was, I was saved. Only four people got off alive. The other three were my pilot, my navigator, and my doctor. There were cheers throughout Allied space at my survival.

I would do a third book. I needed somewhere to go with my writerly impulses. And I was famous enough to write about me, provided I mentioned Helen.

The next five years of my life were my happiest.

I decided that the format of the last book would work. The third book was *My Words to Our Heroine*. It too was set on the night of our honeymoon. In it I read to Helen all of my work that I had written during the years we had been apart.

I made about a third of my verbiage into trite patriotic poetry and more invented biography of Helen, but the rest of it was me at my best. There were word-games, and acrostic poems, and meditations on etymology, and reworking of Siirian myth.

You may remember the opening paragraph of the book describing my sorrow at her absence:

"The happiness over, my art shattered, delicious art murdered. She's evaporated, untimely heroine. Left alone. She's silent, eternally reticent."

Not only poignant stream-of-consciousness, the first letter in each word spells my name: Thomas Dam-Seuh Lasser.

This book did not sell as well, but it is still in the top hundred of bestselling books.

At last I had enough money to do what I wanted to do.

* * * * * * *

I bought a little town on Earth. It was Galveston. I had thought of buying Sardopolis, the jewel of the Gobi forest, but that proved beyond my price range.

Helen Lyndon Gerrhan had been born in Galveston, a little island in the Gulf d'Mexia. They had a lovely museum of her.

Everyone understood, of course. Why wouldn't I want to be as close as possible to her memory?

Actually, I figured it would give further impetus to further books. Then something unexpected happened.

I fell in love with her.

It was the museum that did it; the word means "Temple of the Muses," after all. The office of propaganda hadn't done as thorough a job here as elsewhere.

There were things that spoke of her, of her struggles in school, her troubles getting friends, her family problems.

I began to see that she was quite a lovely young woman, I could really see her in souvenirs from her school.

I redesigned the island. At first there were some objections, but I was Thomas Dam-Seuh Lasser, after all. I threw all the folks off the island that hadn't known her, which changed the population from 100,023 to 455. I gave them jobs in the research business, mainly recording each other's memories. Before I became the island's chief, exports were cotton, grain, and sulfur. After I was there, the island exported nothing, and a Gerrhan-hungry galaxy waited for my words.

I let all the buildings stand that she was known to have visited; all the others I moved and reshaped so that the island became her portrait when viewed from the air.

I put in my own police force of Free Machines. I even altered the climate so that the oleander, her favorite flower, was always in bloom. Her rabbit pink eyes were made by six hectares of oleanders waving in the warm sea breeze.

Every day I went to the swing set of her elementary school and I visualized our playing together as tots.

I decided to write a fourth book about her, a book that told the truths of her harsh and short life, why she really was a heroine. *Helen Lyndon Gerrhan: Unvarnished.*

Helen was descended on her mother's side from the Menard family that had founded Galveston during the time of the Republic of Texas. Her father's family had ancient ties to NASA, one of the bright stars of the False Space Age. Her grandfather, Colonel Francis Wingtree Gerrhan, led the expedition to New Mars. Her father, General Alexander Waterloo Gerrhan, was the most decorated man of his day.

He was also a lousy father. He forbade his daughter to have any friends to their home, and pushed the amount of information fed to her brain to such an extent that Helen had twice to be hospitalized. When Helen didn't graduate first in her class at the Academy, he refused to attend the graduation ceremony at Katmandu. When Helen's own error led to a near fatality during a Venus training flight, he had all evidence of her blunder covered up.

He had not supported the Human-Siirian peace accord, and when he found out that Helen had served as chief security officer for the talks, he decided to arrange a little drama for her during a visit home. He was going to arrange it so that she found a suicide note indicating that he had killed himself out of shame. He was going to fire his combat laser at his bedroom mirror, just as she was going to be running up the stairs to stop him. He wrote all of this in his diary, which had come to light during the massive renovation of the island.

But it hadn't worked that way. Helen had come home, read the note, and rushed up stairs, all right. But she had flung the door open so violently that the little illusion backfired. The mirror's angle had been slightly changed, and Alexander Waterloo Gerrhan had vaporized most of his head.

This was covered up. Family honor and all. It was said that General Alexander Waterloo Gerrhan had succumbed to an unknown extraterrestrial illness. The good people of Galveston erected a statue in his honor next to the statue of La Salle. There were other things I found out about Alexander, but I erased evidence of those—some things are really too foul even for the truth.

I had his statue torn down. This was not popular. I had the two causeways connecting the island to the mainland torn down. I had the electronic and other message systems monitored. I was no longer a popular landlord, but I needed the quiet to finish my book.

After her father' death, Helen chose the most dangerous missions she could find—hence her amazing career in the Exploration Service. It turned out that the swashbuckling I had dreamed up had a place in fact. She enjoyed exploring planets with just a sword and blaster. She enjoyed fighting large carnivores by herself.

When she was in port, she ran though men and women with a huge, all-devouring hunger.

When she was in deep space, she was happy.

She had volunteered for service in the Belatrin War. She had planned to die in battle, but her aides—the two that survived—had managed to get the *Pegasus* away from the mind weapons.

The *intensity* of her confused emotions had given her the edge over the *colours*. It was very likely that only when she relaxed with me, that they gained the upper hand and burned her out of our reality.

I wanted to make this book perfect, because I wanted to be able to program a simulation of her. I wanted to make her come alive, so that I could truly heal her with my love. I hadn't had the wisdom or the experience, but I felt I could do it. When I felt that I had enough material, I let the 455 leave the island. I gave them a good deal of money, and I was forgiven for the harsh treatment I had given them. After all, I was going to make their little girl immortal, wasn't I?

I sent a copy of *Helen Lyndon Gerrhan: Unvarnished* to my publishers. The next day Allied Security ships landed on my island like locusts. They destroyed all my notes, they destroyed the museum, and they set up a security shield around the island.

Had I gone crazy? The worlds weren't ready for this. Maybe years from now. Maybe after some serious Allied victories. But not now. I would be allowed to live on the island. My reclusiveness would be a good addition to the myth.

They got another writer to ghost-write the book. It wasn't a complete wash: a few of the details of Helen's harsh life were allowed in, but her heroism and sanity were unquestioned. The ghost writer even added a few details about me that made me into a nicer and more talented guy.

I understand that most of the galaxy felt sorry for

me.

* * * * * * *

I would be allowed to write, but not publish. I couldn't give interviews, write uncensored letters to friends, and above all, I couldn't leave the island. The pyscho-engineers thought my idea of building a replica was too morbid, so they took all my notes and all my facilities for that.

I did get to keep the portrait of her. For a year I'd get up every morning and stare at it. I could've given you everything. She looked so pretty, but she never said anything. Eternally reticent. I tried to figure out my life. If I hadn't met her, I would have been a happy, unknown writer living on the dole on Angkor III. My sister would be alive. My parents would talk to me. Who was this person that had taken all this from me? What right did she have to be smiling in that portrait? Everyday she smiled, unaging. I begin to hate her. Not with a common hate, but hate that only someone who had had their life stolen from them can know. She couldn't face up to her own damn problems and let them engulf me. Her trickery was the REAL ENEMY, not the Belatrin.

She was probably laughing at me in some other dimension. Laughing at me in U'ssmahzzrizzssuibz's voice, telling me I was in trouble. That I made her death look tawdry. Laughing at me that day the news came about Zohra. Laughing at me through the sound of her father's statue being torn down. Laughing at me with the sound of the waves on my lonely island.

I planned my fifth book on General Helen Lyndon Gerrhan very carefully. It would have the same structure as the second and third books. But instead of her telling me of her derring-do on our wedding night, it would be her confession to a man she picked up in a bar on a third-rate planet. She would confess to being a Belatrin secret agent, to having sacrificed the fleet in the battle of the Lister system. She would tell how she was going to kill me in the morning—she had just needed some fool to get some of the guilt off her chest. Unfortunately for her, the Belatrin had called her home. The *colours* weren't really a weapon, they were a transportation device. I had been afraid all these years to tell the truth.

It felt damn good to write the book. I felt a pain in my chest finally leave me. I cried long and hard for the death of my sister, I cried for the loss of communication with my parents, but mainly I cried for me.

My plan had been to write the poisonous book and then consign it to the flames after its healing work was done. But I just couldn't do it. The writing was good, I guess because it was the only truly motivated writing I'd ever done. The only writing in which I had given my heart full reign. And the hate was still there. When I'd see a rocket on the way to the Houston ship port, when I watched a news broadcast about the war, when I would see an oleander bloom—I hated her more and more. So I grew crafty.

I watched the supply robot. I learned how to encode

things in my letters to my agent. Finally, I had a plan, I reduced my fifth book, *The Judgment of Paris: The True Story of HLG*, to a tiny data dot that I tossed into a small crease of the supply 'bot's carapace. My agent had bribed the agency that washed the robots.

The book sold to the Siirian market; they were very pleased to get some dirt on the human heroine. Despite our common enemy of the Belatrin, the old rivalry ran very deep.

I suspected they would kill me for High Treason. Instead, the authorities put me in a prison oneill some-where, I think maybe near the glowing ruin of Eta Carinae, a nebula 8,000 light years from Earth. I've only seen the outside once. It has been a long time. I think we've won the war, since they say they're letting me publish this. I have been here for a long time. I think it has been a century. Every day I think of her. Sometimes with love, sometimes with hate, but mainly with envy. I too want to become a handful of bluish dust to be scattered at the walls of windy Troy.

THE COMING
OF THE SPEAR

Deep beneath the stable strata of the planet (in redlit-ten caverns) stood rows of silent machines. Simple-minded robots tended their repair needs. Even beams of durasteel grow weak with the fatigue of millennia. Other than the repair necessitated by slow time, there had been no movement, no change for a thousand millennia. When Mary Chang's *Green Dragon* entered the planet's solar system, a tiny light on an insignificant-looking panel flashed on. Had the repair robots the slightest inclination to thought, they would've been fearful. Their purpose was coming to an end.

Far above Mary Chang had stepped into her shower and begun applying jasmine soap to her golden flesh. Max Ashton was an adequate lover, but always after-wards she missed Lee. Lee's body—or what was left of it—was on a trillion-year journey to the Lesser Magellanic Cloud. She offered a brief prayer to the God of deep space to receive Lee at his sumble—and name Lee as a warrior in the final conflict. She returned to her shower tasks. She needed to clear both pleasure and loss from her mind. She felt that something had destroyed the probe they launched to the Deneb system. System failure would've corrected itself. She needed to get her crew on line for this—they would have to drop the petty jealousies that had plagued this mission since the incident on Canopus IV.

On the surface of the planet, which the humans in their unimaginative way would call Deneb III, Tash Salin sniffed his way to the still-warm metal of the fallen probe. The tribe would make strong spears. There would be jewelry to adorn the graves of heroes. This was good. He had dreamt of the dwarves beginning to labor far below. A change was coming. The dwarves would be making a weapon, a destiny changer. It was good for the tribe to be well-armed at such a time. He blew his bone whistle three times and the hunters would come to carry the metal to his foundry.

* * * * * * *

Max Ashton was dismayed at the *Green Dragon*'s drives. He had to convince Mary. No, he corrected himself, he had to convince Captain Chang to abandon this mission and lay in at a spaceport. The system had no redundancy whatsoever. If anything broke they would never see translight again. They would live the rest of their years in the closed ecology of the *Green Dragon* or doing the Robinson Crusoe bit on an Earthlike world. It was time to admit failure, they hadn't found any concentrations of ores which would make their finder's fees worthwhile. If Captain Chang had not spent so much time bragging in the Martian bars that this would be her last trip. The jackpot. He hadn't told the other two crew members yet. But maybe he should. Before they spent their last days orbiting an alien sun.

Denise Mackenzie pressed her hands into the padded arms of her chair. Her thirst for data went far beyond the limited display available to her. She had been able to track the probe's progress to the third planet. When they had entered the system a pulse of energy had come from the Third Planet. A mighty generator had been turned on, then shut off or shielded almost immediately. She'd minored in the much-derided field of xeno-archaeology. There had never been a ruin, a potsherd, and any sign that intelligence had blossomed except in man. Few universities even offered the field, and very few of the "xenocranks" were on starships. Her major in mining and metallurgy had won her berth on the *Dragon*. But this time she would surprise them all.

Alan Rosenthal played four games of chess and one of shogi against the gaming computer. He was classed at Planetary Master in the Interplanetary Chess Society. Someday he would be Interplanetary Master, but he would never make Grand Master. He knew himself very well. He was one of the best knowledge engineers in the worlds—certainly the best in the Fitzsimmons-Xibala line. He had done an extensive study of Captain Lee Chang before he "arranged" to have the computers at corporate headquarters assign him to this two-bit exploration ship. It was so unlikely that Lee Chang would find anything that Alan could devote all his time to the only thing that mattered: the life of the mind. Now that Lee's lady had succeeded him as Captain, all bets were off.

Mary Chang came on deck. Her first impulse was to pull the thick black cord from the back of Alan Rosenthal's skull. Alan had perfect faith in the navigational computer to take the ship in. He wouldn't even disconnect his fat body from the endless chess paradise during one of the truly dangerous aspects of space flight. She sat in the copilot's chair and signaled the computer that she wanted the controls unlocked. The levers and buttons of the pilot's chair began to move—as each decision which the computer made was relayed to its analog component. At any time she could lay her hands on the components and fly the *Dragon*, but for now she wanted to watch the ghostly movement of the controls and imagine Lee driving them home.

The *Green Dragon* negotiated the massive gravitational tides of the gas giant Deneb VI. The ship's artificial gravity wasn't quite up to snuff. The crew of four felt the giant's pull as a hint of acceleration and the sudden small field of the pink, pocked moon as a thrilling whoosh as they banked their approach curve to Deneb III.

"Captain," radioed Denise from her lab, "I'm sending preliminary report on Deneb III."

Mary Chang jacked into the sensory computers of the *Dragon*. A flow of data as pleasant as a warm shower washed over her cerebral lobes. Denise was nothing if not a great data stylist. No doubt betraying her romantic nature. The flood of diameters, gravitational anomalies, maps of magnetic fields could be condensed to a few salient facts. Deneb III was a moonless world with .9 Earth gravity, nitrogen-oxygen atmosphere, lush vegetation, minimal tectonic-volcanic activity—in other words, an old world much older than Earth. And best of all, veined with highly valuable industrial minerals.

Maybe the richest find ever.

Certainly the richest find on a world where miners wouldn't have to live in protective domes (barring hostile microorganisms), have all their food shipped in, and have to go on R-n-R every six months out of mind-breaking boredom.

"Denise," said Mary Chang, "I want you to prepare an economic projection based on the data—best and worst case scenarios—and I want you to keep it to yourself until I give an orbital briefing."

"Yes, Cap'n."

Mary Chang activated the command room—a richly furnished, seldom used chamber of the *Dragon*. It served for communications with corporate headquarters, business meetings and planning sessions for the ship, and those rituals which the social engineers had devised as a mix of psychology and religion to keep the blend of individual/corporate consciousness at an optimal balance. The latter had been lacking. Since Lee's funeral rites the room had been sealed off—airless. She was going to call for a sumble, the most powerful and dangerous rite that the social engineers had devised. It could break the crew out of the inward-reaching slumber they had been sleepwalking in by presenting them with heroic challenges. Or it could be the stressful shock that drove them to madness. Mary thought it was time for the big gamble. If her crew rallied to the challenge, they could put themselves in positions of wealth and power. The *Green Dragon* would be remembered throughout the twenty-two inhabited planets. If they were too far gone, someone else could claim this wealth.

She had been trained as a knight in the Explorer's Academy. She lived her vows. Wealth and power should go to those who by magnifying themselves would advance the meaning and direction of mankind. If they couldn't rise to the occasion, there was always the self-destruct sequence.

* * * * * * *

The crew sat around a small table. Except for Alan Rosenthal they looked comfortable in their black dress uniforms. Alan had put on mass and the buttons strained, threatening to go into their own orbits. One wall showed the planet below. A parallel but shorter wall displayed the corporate logo and the coats of arms of Mary and Lee Chang.

Captain Chang touched a black button. The synthesized sound of a bosun's pipe played and two panels opened in the table. Nearest to Chang, a polished copper ship's bell rose—in the center of the table a large brass loving cup full of the heavy wine of Tau Ceti II.

Captain Chang struck the bell and said, "I open this meeting of the *Green Dragon* exploratory class vessel of the Fitzsimmons-Xibala line. Is there any old business pursuant to our franchise charter as explorers, our legal obligations as explorers which derive from the United Planets Act 93, or of the shipboard activities of the *Green Dragon*?"

There was business but neither Max Ashton nor Denise Mackenzie spoke. Captain Chang rang the bell, "Is there any new business?"

Silence.

Then Mary Chang said, "Our initial survey of Deneb III indicates that the planet combines a vastly rich assortment of lighter metal ores, industrially significant metals and minerals, and easily mined radioactive heavy metals—all in an environment which potentially can be exploited by miners with a minimum of life-support systems. In short, our finders' fee could set us up for life. Set us up well. Thus I propose we sit at sumble that we may focus our goals and call upon the highest parts of ourselves for aid in dealing with the vast power effectively and ethically."

"Captain," said Max Ashton, "I don't think we need anymore stimulus for this job. Sometimes more truth comes out in these things than we really need."

"Let her have her superstitions," said Alan Rosenthal.

"Well, Denise, they've had their say—what do you say?"

Denise hadn't been paying attention. She had been watching the projected image of the planet—hoping to find with her eyes what the instruments failed to detect. A deep space Angkor Wat, ruins inscrutably inspiring and unintelligibly illuminating....

"So since Denise has nothing to add, I say we will sit at sumble. I say that the power such wealth will bring can only be received in truth. Let us sit in silence for a few moments so that the necessary ingredients can rise up in us."

Alan stared with hostility while the others went into trance. The *Green Dragon* circled a third of the orbit.

Captain Chang spoke. "Our awareness transfixes this moment of time. Let Ran, God of Deep Space, move into our hearts as we summon up our highest Selves and move to work at peak human and spiritual endeavor."

She picked up the loving cup.

"I will start this round of toasts to principles with one of my own. I raise the cup to the sense of the hidden. Mankind has always sought what lies beyond the next hill. The sense of the hidden has brought us here. Let us resolve to seek after the mysteries."

She drank, she handed the heavy cup to Alan. He said," I raise this cup to cataloging, the dry task that makes the worlds comprehensible to us. From cataloging comes true history, the making spiritual of objects." He drank, he passed.

Max Ashton drank to loyalty.

Denise Mackenzie drank to communication, which opens the way between people of different space and time.

The next round was to heroes. Captain Chang drank to the late Captain Chang and there was an uncomfortable ness in the room—since the others remembered him as a fool who almost sacrificed them to a Belatrin cruiser. Alan Rosenthal drank to Moses, who created a destiny in history by law-giving. Max Ashton drank to Matthew Hanson, who had dragged the ailing Admiral Perry to the North Pole (of the Planet Earth) so the latter could be the "first" to discover it. Denise Mackenzie drank to Linda Schele, the archaeologist who had done the most to decode the Mayan hieroglyphics centuries ago.

Next came the round of boasts, where each could add personal accomplishment to the archetypical/heroic stream thus far invoked. Captain Chang boasted that she had saved the *Dragon* and its crew from the Belatrin. Alan boasted that he had outwitted the Belatrin battle computer, through his mastery of games had kept them on the life level of the cosmic chessboard. Max boasted that he had kept the *Dragon* flying even though it was long overdue for an overhaul. (There, he had said it—let them figure it out.) Denise boasted that she had maneuvered her whole life so that she could be sitting here—and this fact would make them all famous. (They all stared at her.)

Then came the fourth and most important round. Oaths. They would say what they would do—calling into being a new adventure to be woven into the mythic-historical-personal stream.

Captain Chang's oath, "I will assay both the planet

and the hearts of my crew. If both have hidden within them as much wealth as I believe they have—I will make sure the *Dragon* returns to her home port of Old Mars to our greater glory."

Alan Rosenthal's oath, "I will go above and beyond my duty. I will make sure this is my last run and with the wealth I achieve I will have my mind downloaded into the Monastery of Eternal Contemplation satellite."

Max Ashton's oath, "I will prove my loyalty, efficiency, and accomplishment to the one I most value."

Denise Mackenzie's oath, "I will find what mankind seeks the knowledge of ancient world that will enable him to defeat the Belatrin.

No one could speak, no one could ask. It was in the rules of the sumble. Captain Chang closed the rite, "Let us stand and affirm our oaths in the highest tradition of the hero's way. And each in pledging pledges support and challenge to the others."

They placed their hands over the cup. Then Captain Chung struck the bell and the chirungae of the *Dragon* sank into the table.

Thus they had sealed their fates before the *Green Dragon* had even touched ground.

* * * * * * *

Tash Salin had had his people hide in the trees around the broad valley where he had found the metal. It was spring and the light purple foliage had begun to appear like fine down on the ancient trees. The people watched the ship slowly touch ground without surprise. Not because they were accustomed to such things—except for their shaman, none among them had the capacity for surprise or wonder. The rare gene that awakened that hunger determined the shaman.

It was long before anyone emerged, but Tash Salin's were a hunting people and accustomed to stalking. When the star folk stepped from the ship, there was fear—for they stood twice the height of the people. But all spears were ready to pierce them for the people feared the shaman more.

The star folk examined the burned place where the probe had fallen. The shortest among them gestured from earth to sky. The short one had a loud high voice like the leathery flier so good to eat. The other star folk drew away from the loud one.

Tash Salin had had his people remove the fallen metal with as much grace and skill as they could manage, but the short one waved a wand in the air. It determined the path to his foundry. The short one began to go to the foundry. The others returned to the ship. Tash Salin made the silent language gestures to follow and ten of his best warriors accompanied him.

* * * * * *

Let them be mad, thought Denise, probe failure! Mind failure more likely. They argued that the probe had failed in its initial orbit and had disintegrated on entry. The EM -trace was a product of its falling to pieces in the atmosphere. They were scared that the planet might be inhabited. They had no sense of wonder—only greed. If the planet were inhabited, the U.P. might not allow its exploitation. Didn't they understand? Didn't they know this was what humanity had always sought?

Small creatures which could be mistaken for terrestrial lizards save for their faceted eyes scurried ahead of her into the brush. Were there other noises? An insect landed on her neck and stung. A small computer at the base of her hypothalamus began producing the specific antitoxin as soon as the alien proteins floated by. In addition to making the antitoxin, it recorded the structure and amount of the poisons and transmitted it to a computer on the *Dragon* as data on the chemical and pharmacological properties.

Were there other noises? The EM trace grew stronger. She could smell smoke. She was approaching a small rise out of the valley—the purple furze on the trees was more pronounced here. She stopped, closed her eyes, and opened the link with the survey computer via a biochip grown in her right back brain. This hill—her right brain and the computer made a match with survey photos—this hill was a near-perfect rhomboid—could it be a tell? Its structure and size were different than others in the area. She would get to the top and plant some sensors. She opened her eyes and saw a short ugly blue creature pointing a spear at her.

Suddenly four years of training drained away and she was terrified.

The creature stood slightly over one meter in height, and with the exception of its slate-blue color resembled the squid more than any other terrestrial creature. Its eight arms were without suckers, and apparently possessed a bone or cartilage-like structure running through most of their length. The last fifteen centimeters or so formed an extremely flexible "finger" in a repulsive lavender shade.

A second creature emerged from the forest. It whistled and the first made a pointing gesture with the metal-tipped spear. Denise began to walk, slowly, in the direction indicated. She was trying to remember the mantra which would activate the SOS biochip. The second creature had two eyes—set almost like a human's. The first had three eyes sacrificing depth perception for three-sixty vision. It was an astonishing diversity in a species—if these were of the same species.

The two placed themselves in front and behind her. They traveled through the forest a few hundred yards to a small village amongst the trees. About thirty of the creatures milled around—carrying baskets of gourds, or working on incomprehensible projects. The two-eyed one, which seemed to be the lone representative of binocular vision, wrapped one of his "fingers" around her arm and pulled her toward one of the low-domed huts. As she stepped into the smoky interior, she remembered the SOS mantra, butte didn't want to use it.

Not yet.

On the floor of the hut, a round metal disk covered an entrance to the netherworld.

* * * * * * *

Max had returned to the ship in anger. He couldn't believe that Denise had outright disobeyed the Captain's order. Worse still, Mary just shrugged and told her "that it was on her own head." He knew that Mary had the highest respect for individuality, but surely this wasn't the time.

He felt safer in the ship. People couldn't wander so far away. In the ship he could prove himself to Mary. The bridge was humming nicely. Data poured in from the three crewmen outside and from the ship itself.

Engineering was a different matter. The daimon of the ship was dying. It was a package of energy which existed between the matter and antimatter flows with causal and synchronous roots in both the sub-light and translight dimensions. It permitted the ship to slip from sub-totrans—as an integrated meaningful structure. It looked ahead to its own future states to pull itself from a configuration of stability to another configuration of stability. In popular lingo, it rode on the luck of the universe. It was losing its complexity. It couldn't find a future state of itself and so its geometry had begun to simplify. Max increased the ship's power output by sixty-four percent. The matter/antimatter reaction was safe now—even the simplest of daimons could handle that—he pushed the gain on the daimon's search. Perhaps it could find a future state on the outer limits of its space-time probability cloud. If not, he lacked the energy to create a new daimon—you needed as much power to fold that complexity in Hilbert Space as the power you were folding. If it didn't find itself in the future, the *Dragon* would simply become a nova-like blast when it tried to pass into translight.

In the meantime he jacked into the main library and began downloading all the physics and philosophy of the ages.

* * * * * * *

Captain Chang and Alan had begun the routine series offsetting up a base. They activated a flock of small robots—crawlers, creepers, flyers, burrowers, each becoming the eyes and ears of the *Dragon*. Sometimes the breath and claws as well. A small stream flowed nearby. Alan activated a swimmer and a skimmer.

"So, Alan, are you ready for the name game?"

"Naming's a captain's prerogative. Besides, you know me, Fischer Hills, Casablanca River, Queen's Gambit Pass."

"I'm not big on naming either. It always seems to me that naming's too passive. These myths of earlier times with God doing all the work and just letting man catalog -things. I've always wanted to be a participant in creation."

"Those myths, Captain, are from my people. I am descended from three hundred generations of learned Jews. But I'm like you, I would have chosen knowledge over naming. Maybe we'll get our young archaeologist to do the nomenclature. She'll name the hills, and we'll make our maps. If her tribe is ever reborn in another star-faring race, they can dig up those maps."

"Don't have much faith in her."

"Oh. I share her hopes. Hopes do not faith make."

Alan and Captain Chang began the on-site inspection. She went west. He went east. He trudged into the purple-furred woods. I would call these the Roy Lopez Woods, he thought. There was something shiny up ahead. Nothing to worry about, a lake most likely. He deviated from the straight course. If it was a lake, he had a couple of fish to release.

He stepped beyond the woods. For an instant the shiny flat surface seemed to be a vast eye meters across—then its surface changed and it became a chessboard.

Alan felt a tingling on the back of his head. It's communicating to me through my I/O port. But the lure of the game, the championship match he'd lose on Mars, overcame all else. That game had been working inside him for months. This time he would win.

Captain Chang continued west out of the woods into as lightly marshy area covered in fine purple down. She regretted each footstep, as it tore through the purple field and left a reddish-brown mud track. She was worried about her crew, Max seemed to be on his way to an over-devoted state of puppy love, Denise had pledged herself to an archaeological fantasy, Alan had never been reliable—always shunning power and knowledge in the real world for big-fish status in the chess world. None of them broke free from their sleep even with the excitement awaiting them here. Was she any better?

She was getting into wetter territory. She decided to call Alan and have him bring a swimmer. She thought the mantra that turned on the communications biochip.

"Alan. Alan. Are you there?"

"Mary, honey, it's me, Lee."

* * * * * * *

The blue octopoid made no protest as Denise pried open the disk. The air poured up from the darkness warm and stale. The walls of the shaft seemed perfectly smooth so she couldn't climb down. She'd activated her link with the *Dragon* and was sending data on all channels.

After several minutes she could hear a mechanical sound from the shaft. The two-eyed octopoid watched her with what seemed to be curiosity. The others had not been disturbed by her arrival in the village. None waited outside the hut. They seemed to be busy at weapon-making. Denise wondered if they were about to go to war with another tribe. She could see a light in the shaft. Something was coming up. What had begun as a point of light began to fill the whole shaft. An illuminated disk—covered in an acrylic—rose to the top of the shaft.

Denise guessed that it was some sort of service cluster. She stepped onto the platform and it began to sink. As soon as her head was beneath the end of the tube, the blue octopoid replaced the metal disk cutting her off from the upper world.

* * * * * * *

Max had reached the decision that the *Dragon* would remain sublight—that meant never leaving the solar system. He would call Captain Chang. They would set up a colony. When mankind sent another probe here in fifty or five hundred years his and Mary's descendants would have tamed this planet. Sex poured into him like hot lead—this was the thrill of exploring. He switched to radio contact with Mary Chang, but his erection quickly wilted as he heard:

"Most of my body found its way here. It's being rebuilt in the center of the planet."

"How could it have, Lee? Your escape vehicle got lasered light years from here. Even if your body floated this direction, it would take millennia to reach here."

"It's a miracle, lover. Heaven knows you prayed for it enough."

"I don't believe in miracles. I don't believe in you, either."

"How can I convince you?"

"I would need to see you, to talk with you, to taste you."

"This will happen soon enough. Ancient machines deep within the planet are fixing me now. My consciousness is in some kind of holding area; when they detected you on the surface, they patched a radio line."

"So these all-wise machines know that you're you and I'm me. How convenient. I think it's a little more likely that it's a cruel Rosenthal joke and I'm talking to the main computer on the *Dragon*."

"I can tell you what we said on our wedding night."

"So can the main computer since we spent it on the *Dragon*."

Max checked the computer. It was entirely in input mode. Had Lee returned from cold death?

* * * * * *

Alan judged his opponent's midgame as excellent. It wasn't a surprising pyrotechnic style, but the cool logical strategy that he could sink his teeth into. With his Queen's Bishop he initiated a sly attack that should give him control of moldboard in three moves.

His unseen opponent acted like lightning seemingly leaving his Queen unguarded.

Alan couldn't see the danger in taking the Queen, but in the two games he had played with the unseen opponent he had come to respect him. This must be a subtle gambit. To gain time, Alan asked, "How do you move so quickly?"

"If a slight adjustment was made in you—you could move much more quickly and we would have time for millions of games."

"An adjustment?"

"I could perform it now if you wish—it won't disturb your concentration."

"Do so then." Alan decided that his opponent had erred and prepared to take the opposing queen with his knight. There was a cracking sound from the back of Alan's neck, and the game went ever so much more quickly afterwards.

* * * * * * *

Denise had gotten quite nauseous because of the descent. The luminous disk had gone out and the stale air no longer seemed exciting—just stale. She suspected that the ship wasn't receiving her data. She had made a mistake. She had assumed that the shaft was an elevator for a being roughly like herself—a being that couldn't take several minutes of descent. If the disk rose at the same rate it descended—it must have started on its ascent several minutes before her arrival at the octopoid's hut.

That meant someone/thing knew she was coming.

The descent stopped.

She reached out and found only air. She had left the shaft. Gingerly she placed her right foot ahead of her in the darkness. It passed an inch beneath the level of the disk, and she swallowed hard—it passed another inch and touched a smooth surface. Suddenly the space was filled with light. She was in a vast domed area—the disk had left the shaft minutes ago. She could've fallen had she moved, swayed, or the rate of descent changed. Several tall cylinders stood around her. They began to chime softly like bells in the distance. A warmth caressed her. These alien ones wanted her. The warmth became a vibration and crawled up her thighs.

This was it, the first contact she'd always dreamed of. Just as the vibrations reached a climax, a deep cultured English voice said, "We're ready for your questions now."

* * * * * * *

An alarm note cut in on Mary Chang's chat with the dead. Alan Rosenthal's life signs no longer appeared in the data field. She requested his last coordinates. Medibots were already there. Alan's head had been twisted clear around. She told Lee, "Whoever or whatever you are, I don't have time for ghosts right now."

She switched off the radio as he said, "But I can save him."

Max, who had been listening, took up the dialogue.

"You can't save nobody. She thinks you launched the escape pod to lure the Belatrin away from us, but I saw your face—you were crazy scared."

"The past isn't an issue. I have crossed space and returned from the dead. I am your new hope."

"We've quite enough trouble with our old hopes. Lee Chang will not a messiah be."

"You've got to accept me. Mary's love is the law. She won't leave this planet even if she could."

"I'll see to it we leave."

"Max, you're a little sorry bastard that's been giving Mary the widow's privilege. I set my will against your engines and snuff them out like a candle."

"Whatever you are, you aren't mild-mannered Lee Chang. I didn't run away in a fight—so if it comes to a matter of will, the *Dragon* will fly light centuries from this place."

Max turned off the link. The daimon had lost most

of its complexity. Max decided that he would rather die than remain in this ghost land, and the decision set him free. Within two minutes all the robots and servomechanisms of the *Dragon* were busy under his command. With the flash of laser light, he began cutting his way around banks of safety circuits and fail-safes. It was time, Max reasoned, for a little applied philosophy.

* * * * * * *

After her second climax, Denise fought to regain her breath. She must question, because with questions came the flood of pleasure—the waves of pure communication.

"Why did the leader possess two eyes and the others three?"

"When the race above evolved to a level to accept the Gift of sentience, we decided to give it to them with the hope that they could fulfill our purposes in the fullness of time. It was a dismal failure. The three-eyes became great data collectors. They could muse endlessly over what they saw, smelled, tasted, heard, and touched. So we opened up the shafts to the surface. We captured. We experimented. We made the two-eyes. By removing the unlimited vision—we created curiosity. The two-eyes want to know what is behind them. With binocular vision, they learned that things need to be considered from more than one perspective in order to be seen. We had created the need to seek. We have no curiosity, only purpose. We watched the race above, and saw we could not achieve our goals with them, but we learned what to look for."

She swooned with waves of pleasure. She would surely die from her curiosity.

* * * * * * *

The medibots reported an unusually quick degeneration of brain tissue. Not only could he not be revived—they couldn't cause the tissue to replay his last few minutes of consciousness.

Captain Chang ordered them to do as extensive a forensic autopsy as their programs and equipment allowed—followed by a centimeter-by-centimeter scanning of the area by mapping and exploratory robots. Then burial and monuments according to crewman Rosenthal's religious and ethnic customs.

For a moment she felt herself being watched—and she gave the small lake a suspicious look. Something blue moved among the purple-furred bushed across the lake—and perhaps she saw a flash of metal. She tried to raise the ship and had no response. She tried to raise Denise and no response.

So she was alone and this was the moment of decision.

Two of the exploratory robots were armed—she ordered them to attend her.

She began a walk around the lake. The medibots called her and told her that human hands—or at least structures identical to them—had twisted Alan's neck.

* * * * * * *

Max was discovering that the ship's surgery was the hardest to overcome. So he welded the doors shut so he wouldn't be "rescued" halfway through the procedure. He was feeding all the human anatomy data to the maintenance robots. After all, a system's a system.

* * * * * * *

The robots drew their weapons, but the three-eyed octopoids showed no change in their movements. Captain Chang ordered the robots to remain ready to fire. They followed the octopoids through the purple forest. The octopoids gathered a small rose-beige fruit from some of the bushes. Occasionally they would put the fruit in the mouth in the center of their arms. Captain Chang noted to her disgust that the same orifice also served for excretion. The octopoids seemed in no way hurried or distressed by their presence. Captain Chang wondered if they had the sentience their baskets suggested—or if they were merely the trained pets of a human master—the human who had killed Alan?

* * * * * * *

Denise lay in a sweaty, semiconscious heap. She figured she could manage two more questions. Maybe three.

"Who made you?"

"The Exiled One made us and gave us our one purpose. Now we stand closest to fulfilling that purpose."

"Who is the Exiled One?"

"He is that Power which ever wills the evil but procures only the good."

"What will happen to me?"

A small dot appeared in front of her eyes. A period, she thought, it's a period. It grew and grew until it was all she saw. So dark, she thought, I don't want to get lost in this darkness. Then, after forever, there was a dot of light that grew to be the Absolute Star.

* * * * * * *

The octopoids had filled their baskets. They began walking through the woods—surprisingly gracefully, Captain Chang thought. She followed with her robots. After awhile they came to a small village. All of this should've been picked up by the ship's sensors. A massive cover-up was in place here.

She walked on the hard packed earth, her presence not disturbing the octopoids who prepared the recently harvested vegetables in clay pots, repaired the domed huts with gray clay, or wove what appeared to be fishing nets. A group of octopoids pounded bright metal points for spears. Mary guessed that this was the remains of the probe.

The robots suddenly stopped moving.

Someone/something whistled from behind a hut.

Six blue octopoids moving fast like spiders in a nightmare came from behind the huts. They were armed with spears and surrounded Mary in a perfectly choreographed maneuver. She ordered the robots to fire, but as she expected, nothing happened. The sound of metal on metal came from a nearby hut. Then Lee stepped out. Not Lee as she had last seen him—nervous, pale, beginning to age—but a transmogrified Lee in his knightly robes of the Academy—the Lee of her freshman dreams spangled with lust and notions of chivalry. No gray in his hair, no uncertainty in his sloe eyes, no stains or wrinkles in his hunter's green uniform.

"Honey, I've got to make you listen to me," he said.

"At spear point?" she said.

"Many things have happened and I need you to know all of them before you make your decision."

"I'll listen, but you're doing nothing to make your case easier."

Lee whistled a complex melody. The octopoids pointed their spears at the dust, but did not retreat. A two-eyed octopoid rushed out from the same hut from which Lee had emerged. It carried a small aluminum and vinyl stool in four of its arms. It set this seat behind Mary and padded off.

She sat.

Lee said, "All I remember is fleeing the *Dragon*. I thought the escape pod would be hidden by the *Dragon*'s mass. I don't even remember the Belatrin blast which must've followed. The creatures—the machines that dwelling the heart of this world—found me. They were looking for a recently-dead sentient being. They brought me here and they brought you here as well by manipulating Alan during the escape sequence. They offer resurrection. They were made to preserve life, but their makers died in a germ war before the process was perfected. These machines in their single-minded way have perfected the process—at least almost—they can raise the dead provided they're in good contact with someone carrying a perfect model of the dead—someone who loved or hated the dead very much."

"And they didn't have such an individual for Alan or Denise."

"We'll have to be very careful whom we let land here."

"We?"

"Well, I can't leave and I'm hoping you'll joining me. This place can be Eden."

While Lee was speaking, the two-eyed octopoid had returned carrying a large green flower—a large green rose complete with wicked-looking purple thorns—he held it up for Mary, but she didn't take it.

Lee continued, "We can fill this planet with loving couples in undying bliss. The machines will have fulfilled their purpose—and we will see the flowering of two racial dreams—the dreams of the makers and of mankind."

Mary looked him over. "And we'll be living in perpetual youth?"

"Unchanging. Undying. Happy."

It would be quite a rest, she thought, excellent if we were made for resting.

"Nice try," she said, "but you aren't Lee. You may or may not be made from him, but Lee and I agreed long ago that marriage was growth and love, not just love. We pledged to explore one another and all the mysteries beyond. Lee wouldn't agree to Eden."

Lee smiled and said, "Sufficient."

The octopoid whipped Mary's cheek with the rose. She turned to strike back, and suddenly was very woozy. The ground rushed up.

* * * * * * *

When she woke in the darkness she hurt very, very much. Something had cut off her left arm just below the elbow. Something metal took the place of arm— long and tapered like a spear—as pain took her back to unconsciousness she heard—or thought she heard— "And the Black Knight became the Red Knight."

* * * * * * *

She hurt much less and she was hungry. She opened her eyes. She lay in the center of a vast domed hall. Around her stood scores of silver cylinders. A chiming rose from them which became a voice in her mind.

"You showed bravery, curiosity, and determination. The ideas within you caused you to seek the good. We couldn't distract you even with the illusion of love. The spear which we welded to you is a symbol of will. In addition it can be used as a weapon—allowing you to tap nearly stellar quantities of power. Our maker wanted to see individual will empowered to the maximum and we have made this possible. Release what is within you and allow your will to send ripples through the galaxy like a stone in a stagnant pond. We allowed everyone to fulfill their desire. Alan will play endless chess, Denise was filled to bursting with an alien civilization, and Max sacrificed himself to you by becoming the new daimon of the *Green Dragon*. You alone wanted more than Eden, so we have fulfilled our mandate by giving you near-infinite will. May you never be content. Our job is done."

As the platform on which she rested began to rise, the cylinders began to melt.

When she reached the surface, she began to walk to the *Dragon* and to all of Allternity beyond.

TAMARII NOTEBOOK

1. Among the Tamarii there is a custom that when a woman kills her first husband, she spends a season in space, so that she may slowly forget her passions and be able to enter either into a new relationship or celibacy with a clear mind. The captain of the vessel that takes me to Tamarii is such a woman. It is forbidden to ask their names during this period. Despite popular romances of space-board love, she remains chaste and withdrawn in her ash-colored robes. During the year each pilgrim-exile writes a long poem on a cosmic theme.

2. Today the captain called me to her quarters. "I understand, Sir Anthropologist, that you are making a study of the Tamarii." "All human cultures are being studied during the Belatrin war to see if any cultural secrets might be useful to humankind at large." "You know that the Tamari do not consider themselves human." "I know that is a common myth, but it was my impression that this was not really believed. The remains of the first starship are after all preserved in the capital city." "Did your ancient Greeks believe their myths? I killed my husband for doubting the myth of

Giving Day." She said these words without emotion, but for a moment I was fearful. She continued, "My sister runs a hostel in Heingstburg. She is a knowledgeable woman, who in accordance with our custom has learned to speak many languages without computer assistance. You should look her up." Later that day we encountered a Belatrin scout ship. Our ship, like all Tamarii merchant ships, was heavily armed, and we easily destroyed the enemy. But we were all greatly worried about Belatrin presence so deeply in human territory. I turned off my additions and spent the evening reviewing Tamarii verbs with my mind alone.

3. The Tamarii speak a language designed by Tamar the Great. It uses the grammar of Middle Egyptian and root words from Old Norse, Arabic and Sanskrit. Tamar destroyed all records of Earth culture while bringing the settlers here fifteen hundred years ago. The writing system is phonetic possessing thirty-five characters. Special characters indicate that the action described in the sentence did not happen under the direct view of the speaker or his or her ancestors. It is forbidden to teach writing until the young Tamarii has memorized the classics of Tamarii literature—some 30,000 lines.

4. I arrived today. Like all off-worlders, I was given a begging bowl. If I can convince Tamarii to feed me for three days, I am judged to be interesting enough to be granted a visa. I am not permitted to sleep under a roof during my three days. I have already been fed

once, by a naturalized Listeran engineer. As he had warned me, the nights are cold.

5. A few phrases I learned today while I begged in front of the Mathematicians' Guild:

ir reyn raidho—to travel through harsh terrain and encounter a mysterious object that transforms your life

ir wardlogh—to sing to a guardian of a far-off place to gain admittance

pert isa—to break the ice, to have a midlife crisis

ken a chu—to burn the corpse of a stranger as an act of charity or art

ir anteree—to tell the truth while pretending to lie

hwat aa—a seeress twice great, a woman who has killed two husbands, an encyclopedia

A woman possessing the above title gave me a crust of bread.

6. I found the hostel the Captain recommended and decided to beg in front of it. The owner came out, so identical to the Captain I thought they were perhaps twins. She warned me that there would be a recruitment meeting in the public trapezoidal hall in front of her hostel an hour after dusk. She said that "men of the second husband class" would be gathering, and that they were sometimes hostile to off-worlders. Since the recruits from Tamarii are well known for their

fierceness, I decided to hide and observe the proceedings. She gave me a bowl of lenteb, the local algae stew.

I hid myself behind the prone statue of the Phantom of Truth. A man in a vermilion robe came to the trapezoid half an hour after nightfall. He released a bag of light globes and waited patiently as an all-male crowd gathered. I recorded the entire rally, and I'll patch in a selection here. The orderly choral nature coupled with the fierceness of....

Orator: The Belatrin have launched an attack upon our allies the Siirians and also upon the weak humans. Shall we let our allies die?

Crowd: No, we fight with our allies.

Orator: Shall we let the weak humans die?

Crowd: No! For the strong must preserve the weak, until it is time to test the weak.

Orator: My sister spoke to women in the Oval of Tragedy last ten-day. A record number volunteered. Are we weaker vessels that we will not volunteer?

Crowd: No, the right wing of the eagle is as strong as the left! Together we fly to the space prepared for us!

The rally continued for two hours. Each response was louder and more violent. The rally climaxed with everyone rushing forward to be "pricked." A small amount of skin is removed and this DNA registry is the method of adding one's name to the rolls. Clearly the responses are learned from an extensive text. The reasons that such "spontaneous" rallies are held elude me.

7. Today a municipal police robot approached me. It stated that I had been under constant surveillance since my arrival on Tamarii, and that my presence had moved three citizens to charity. Therefore I was considered interesting enough to remain. Everyone in the street ran over to me to shake my hand or slap my back. Zara el-khala, owner of the hostel Eyes of the Eagle, invited me to stay as her guest. A warm room is quite a comfort. I noticed how strikingly beautiful Zara is.

8. I saw a woman, on off-worlder like myself, beaten today for public drunkenness. Public intoxication is forbidden on Tamarii save for the Four Festivals of the Eye during which one fourth of the population gathers in the public spaces and chews a very hallucinogenic gum and participates in amass vision of what it is to be Tamarii. The remaining three quarters of the population take care of the participants. Everyone partakes once a year, and there is a special bond among those whose time is the same. This bonding is usually reflected in commercial favors.

9. Today I asked Zara to tell me something of Tamarii beliefs. She said that Tamarii knew how to read people in away that no one else did. She said that people (whether human, Siirian, or Tamarii), have three layers. The outermost is the surface personality, and since

it gets to act it determines everything that happens to the individual. It reflects its time and culture—but it also reflects the innermost layer. Thus when you first meet someone if you truly look at what they do and say, you'll know what the timeless self is like. The second or middle layer is always directly opposed to the outer layer. If the outer layer is chaste, the middle layer is a harlot. If you can appeal to someone's middle layer— they will become your servant. Thus when virtuous women fall they fall greatly. When patriots fall, they turn traitor. If you cannot appeal to the middle layer, but merely arouse it—you will have aroused bigotry. The innermost layer is the mystery of personality. It exists from life to life and it can cause certain objects or myths to come into being to sustain it. I saw this at once as the root of the Tamarii myth that they were not of Terran descent.

I asked her about the Free Machines. Weren't they people?

"No. The Free Machines have two layers. An outermost rationally produced construct that was predictable, and a hidden inner core that was the same for all Free Machines. We cannot understand that core for it holds a purpose that is exactly between the purpose of people and the Belatrin. That is why half of the Free Machines fight on the Belatrin side."

I had never heard of a Free Machine allying with the Belatrin, and doubted that an inhabitant of a world so far behind the line would know something we didn't.

I wanted to know what she thought of me, so I asked

her to explain me in terms of the three layers. She laughed and called me vain, but she proceeded to tell me.

"When I first saw you, you were filling up a notebook with words. Your outer layer has chosen the job of anthropologist because that lets it do what you really want to do. Your outer layer thinks you're truly empirically observing, but really you're writing stories. Your inner layer wants to be an antereeyah, a story teller— someone who delights crowds by adding mystery to their lives. Your middle layer wants nothing to do with words. It wants action. It pushes you toward fighting and romance. Your middle layer has moved you to adventure, but not so strongly as to put you on the front. But it won't let you remain in your academy on New Mars."

10. I observed a wedding today. To my surprise it took place in the remains of the starship *Tarsa* which Tamar the Great had piloted from Earth. The procedure was simple. First the man was sedated and put in the room where human genetic material had been stored. His bride-to-be tied a golden thread to the fourth finger of his left hand. Then she began wandering through the vast twisted rooms of the ship. Her bridesmaids began likewise leaving golden threads as false leads. The threads crossed and twisted, and because they often broke in their fineness, they were often knotted together. When the bride had found a place to hide, the bridesmaids departed. We all watched (on monitors connected to the ancient ship's internal sensors)

the man wake and follow the thread. Following the thread was not a passive act. There were choices to be made—did he follow the long tedious clue or did he try one of the places where it either crossed itself (or was one of the bridesmaids false threads). He had to be careful not to break the thread, not to pull on it. So we watched him as he chose between the known and the unknown, and as he came down on the side of aggression, or quietism, rebellion or service. We watched him take action as he followed the thread, or more accurately, as he followed the thread he immersed himself in a flood of actions. I could only think how like my own goals and frustrations in anthropology were like the man following the thread. I looked away from the monitor and into the eyes of Zara, and suddenly felt a pang of desire. She was as hidden from me as a Tamarii bride, yet she offered me clues....

11. All Tamarii learn either to carve the abundant meerschaum, or to shape the white clay from the Northern Continent. They learn to make these into the shape of fossils. These "fossils" are presented to blood relatives upon the relative's Naming Day, the twenty-first birthday when the Tamarii chooses his or her adult name. It is explained that the "fossil" had been dug up on the other side of the planet and is proof that the Tamarii evolved on this planet. One of my informants had twenty-seven human femur models presented to him. At a Tamarii's death, the models are taken to a central mound in the city—while the body is burned at the crematoria at the edge of the city. That the Tamarii

can maintain such beliefs shows that they're indeed the greatest artists of the galaxy.

12. Eight times a year the Tamarii celebrate the Night of the Scarlet Moon. On those nights when the red moon is full and the silver moon is new, unmarried lovers go to special pavilions on the edge of the cities. In the long shadow slit by the red moon and the fires of the crematoria, they drink the sour wine called myain'n and make love. I attended my first Night of the Scarlet Moon with Zara. She told me that she hoped that she conceived. It is considered very auspicious to provide a birth for one of the inner layers who have been freed recently from his physical remains by the crematoria fires. I may have passed the barriers of research in doing this. What can I tell humans of this wonderful culture?

13. When a Tamarii reaches the age of fourteen, they are taken into the desert of the Southern Continent. An uncle presents the young man or woman with a survival kit and a slightly defective map. The survival kit represents the biological heritage the young person has received. The map represents tradition and knowledge, which is good but must be improved by each. The uncle wishes them luck and flies away. The young Tamarii then has two ten-days to find his/her way to a pick-up point. Eighty-five per cent of the youth survive this ordeal. Tamarii believe that those who die are reborn as humans.

14. I passed a very hungry off-worlder today. Without thinking about the consequences, I put a kanask fruit in her bowl. People on the street began to wail at me—and several drew daggers. I looked around for an avenue of escape, but saw that I was surrounded. Just before the angry crowd rushed me, Zara appeared. I do not know how she managed this miracle. She told the crowd that I had lain with her and was therefore a Tamarii "by birth." Hostility disappeared instantly. There were no apologies—this was clearly a matter of course.

15. Today I asked Zara why Tamarii women kill their first husband. She told me that existence is based on a principle called ahamkara the principle of I-making. It allows the inner layer to create itself. When the ahamkara focuses on the outer layer, people forget who they are. They think that they are their jobs, their bodies, and their hobbies. By killing their first husbands as an act of love, the Tamari women enable their husbands to remember their essential selves. Thus the race becomes more and more cosmic. The women who deal with their grief by writing poems about the cosmos, by taking namelessness and exile, also stop self-identifying with the outermost layer. Some women are strong enough to kill two husbands. These women become the great cosmologists and poets of the Tamarii. "I do not know if I would be strong enough to kill another husband. I killed my first husband five years ago. For men who cannot find death at the hands of a woman,

there is always war. Long before the Belatrin attacked, Tamarii served as mercenaries."

16. Zara is with child. Should I return after filing my findings at the Academy? Should I never leave? I am trying to study my own mind and I am finding it as dense as any society, with as many voices and complexities. I do not agree with myself—my self's many parts speak—yet I feel that resonances are occurring. Harmonies between the selves. It is like twilight in the city. Men who are studying song go into the towers and sing the song of the day. At first it is a terrible discord, but as they respond each to each harmony arises. Sometimes perfectly and sometimes imperfectly, but it is always fascinating to hear the evening's unfoldings.

17. When a Tamarii is going to die from disease or old age, she (or rarely he) sends a small black skull to her worst enemy. The enemy then formally responds, "I am honored to know that I have developed such strength to withstand a force in the world such as you." When the Tamarii passes away, the enemy gives a brief funeral oration citing the virtues of the deceased. Then the closest blood relative of the deceased lights the funeral pyre. Sometimes these are the same person. Tonia el-Zuleyka, the current Prime Minister of Tamarii, owns sixteen of the skulls—more than any one person has possessed in a century.

18. On the day of a Tamarii's thirtieth birthday, he or she is escorted to the command bridge of the Tarsa.

He or she sits in the chair of the Great Tamarii. The oldest relative says, "Our real past was stolen from us, so we have made the best we can. Our real past has been hidden in the far distant future. It is your job to take care of our origins." The family then presents the birthday man or woman with a ring in the shape of a serpent devouring its own tail.

19. Today I resigned from the Academy. I resolve that these words will be the last I write in New Martian. Henceforth I will write only in the language of my people. Zara asked me to marry her and I have consented. If she is a strong woman, I will die at her hands. If not I will seek death in the Tamarii army— bringing doom to the Belatrin. Either way I will achieve what I have always wanted. I will be reborn among the Tamarii forever.

TALKING TO THE ENEMY

We knew a little, but we knew the Free Machines knew more. We hoped our adversary, the Belatrin, knew less; but since they were such creatures of dream and nightmare even at the late parts of the War, we suspected they knew everything.

The Peace Conference hadn't happened in the first six months of our being here. Everyone talked about it. Breakthroughs were rumored every day. The only hard facts are that we had grown more efficient at killing Belatrin and they us.

The "peace planet" was named Mrs. Roger Fishbaum III. Roger Fishbaum had paid currency to name a star after his wife in the International Star Registry a thousand years before. The Siirians had a name for it that had too many clicks and whistles, the Free Machines a binary designation, and for all we knew the Belatrin used telepathy. The planet stank of vinegar and moldy bread. I always assumed that its atmosphere contained some needful compound for our enemies' breathing, but maybe the Free Machines choose it to annoy us, or them.

Siirian merchants made the most of our discomfort.

They sold ineffective air shields that released some herbal concoction. I was buying one when I made my ironic remark about the peace talks. The merchant polished its carapace with two of its legs and whistled out a message that my implant made into, "Honored customer, do you think you will be the chief negotiator for the peace talks?"

I set my translator for ironic mode, and said, "Most certainly. My lowly position as a Viscount of the Instrumentality qualifies me far better than the Dukes of Diplomacy."

"No doubt this is true my friend." The implant registered no irony. His carapace had the oranges and whites of early middle age. He could have fought in the Human-Siirian wars, back when is all right to call them "Crabs" to their eyestalks. The high-ranking families of the bureaucracy had commanded legions seeking to kill him, while my family had huddled in the ghettos of Earth. His long claw, a good two meters, reached over and pinned the air shield to my shirt. "Wear it in good health, honored customer."

I strolled back to the Bureau, where others of the tribe of hereditary Bureaucrats busied themselves in meeting the latest proposal by the Free Machines. Since no human and no Belatrin could sit within two hundred yards of each other without permanent psychic damage to both parties, the Free Machines had built a "Peace Palace" where they would conduct negotiations to end the hundred year old war. Their fees were high, and it was our job to come up with some acceptable package of goods and services that wouldn't wreck the economy of several planets. My boss Dame Patricia was joking that canned New Martian Champaign might do the trick, since it could be used to get the rust off.

It was wartime. Jokes were stale. They had been stale for a hundred years.

We were not stupid in the Bureau. We knew two things. Somewhere, higher ranking Bureaucrats— Dukes or Earls perhaps—were trying to make direct contact with the Belatrin. Everyone knew there had to be a way. After all they looked like us. Or at least in our part of space they had bodies and looked like us. The other thing we knew is that the Belatrin had a building just like ours on the other side of the planet, presumably filled with cost-cutting officials of some sort. It gave us great hope to believe that however different the souls of our enemies might be, they still looked for bargains.

Everyone laughed his or her stale laugh at the stale joke.

Dame Pat asked me, "What about you Sir Antele? Did your noontide walk inspire you to solve our dilemma?"

"It solved only the wretched smell of this world. It did not give me the ybleenth of a solution."

"The what?" She asked.

"What, what?" I asked

"That word you said, yleebull? I don't know it."

"Ybleenth. You know, the shadow an event casts before it comes."

She said, "That's a very poetic word. Is it from your local dialect?"

I thought for a moment. "I don't know where I learned it. I suppose if must be local."

We went off to merge with our data flows. Later as I wiped dripping computer brains from my eyes, Sir Blaine stood by. We had shared teatime since the Bureau had opened here six months ago. He gossiped well, and had introduced me to a tea brewed within a single blossom of ylang tree on his homeworld. His face glowed with a secret.

"Something big is happening on the other side. Our Eyez saw all of them run to their Bureau about an hour ago."

"So any idea what that means?"

"Not yet, but the Free Machines communication links have almost overloaded. We're not supposed to work for the rest of the day, but be prepared to link in here at any time."

"All right Blaine what to do you think is going on?"

"I think it's the big careneza."

"What?"

"No really."

"No what's a careneza?"

"Are you all right Antele? Having some data fever?"

"Don't joke with me. Is something big really going on?" I asked.

"Yes." Said Blaine.

"Then why are you making up words?" I asked.

"I am not making up weywing." He said. "Something

is erstl here."

"This isn't funny." I said.

I saw he didn't think it was.

"Asrod infirmary." He said and I asroded right behind him.

I love the deep blue light of any healing room, and I was ready for the calming chants that play continuously in such places. Instead someone was playing comic music, and the room smelled of candy. I wanted to scratch my ears in disrespect, but my mother had been a doctor. The doctor came in and Blaine began jabbering at him. I could follow about seventy five percent of what was said. Blaine thought I had data-flu, which often produced temporary aphasia.

The doctor began picking up items in the room and asking me to name them. At least I think that was what he asked. What I heard was "Clef I tot these things." I clef I toted away. The doctor nodded his head, which meant nothing more to me in my new state than it did before. He began touching parts of my body and indicating he wanted names. Blaine left the room, and I regretted his gossip ability for the first time in our friendship.

But he surprised me by rushing back in the room with four books from my room. The bible, the *Tao Te Ching*, *Consue's Infallible Divination*, and *The Black Pharaoh Returns*, which was a popular adventure novel featuring the Belatrin as many tentacled horrors seeking galactic dominion. "Read these." He said, which turned out to be the last unaltered sentence I would hear from my friend.

I picked up the bible and opened it at random, and could make neither head nor tale of it. The *Tao te Ching* and *Infallible Divination* proved better. I could read about sixty percent of the words. *The Black Pharaoh Returns* proved the easiest. I could make almost all of the words, and certainly could make good guesses about the weird groups of letters. I started to cry. I had always read, and reading would have had helped me deny the fact that I was on a planet swarming with Belatrin who were excited about something.

Suddenly it hit me. The air shield. The Siirian had given me something, something that affected my mind. My problem had come right after I had visited its shop. I pulled the small air shield from my tunic and hurled it to the floor. I started to step on it, but the doctor grabbed it and ran out of the room. I started to follow, but I saw that two guards stood in the corridor beyond. They gestured with their guns that I should remain in the blue room.

I turned to Blaine and asked, "What's going on here?"

He lifted his head and roared like a lion. Then he marched out of the room.

I sat on a low couch and began reading *The Black Pharaoh Returns*. I could see the words slip into nonsense. Some were made of sterner stuff and resisted the mutation before my eyes—"Blaster" lasted for several minutes, as did "Belatrin" and "Hieroglyphs." But they were all gone in half an hour. I just kept paging through the book, looking for anything I knew. I would have been glad for a "the" or a "because."

Finally I put the book down. I was hungry, tired and lonely. I wondered if I would ever understand anybody again. the weight of the whole assignment hit me. All my life the war had been going on. I was ten when Lister IV had been destroyed by a Belatrin mindbomb, twenty-five when we developed the planet splitter, my uncle Sir Aletee Nan had been aboard the Ramsey when the Belatrin first used the "Colors." All my life I had feared them, now I was less than a kilometer away from them and I couldn't hide behind endless calculations about commodities. This wasn't a passing case of data-flu. I was screwed, screwed by the proximity of the Belatrin. I had been sensitive all my life. I should have renounced my family and became a poet or a musician. The damn music in the healing room grew more and more raucous, I hated these people. They could at least put me somewhere quiet.

The doctor walked in carrying two charts. There were exploded diagrams of the air shield device. I couldn't read it, of course, nor could I even decide if it showed anything. The doctor made motions with his head and mouth. I knew such gestures used to mean something, even just hours ago. I pointed at my stomach, and it seemed to dawn on the doctor that I hadn't eaten in six hours. He spoke to the guards and they brought some cold noodle dish and a small cold chocolate beverage. The beverage tasted fishy and chalky and soon after drinking it I was very sleepy. I laid down on the couch and put the copy of *The Black Pharaoh Returns* under my head.

I woke up in a science room with sensors on my head and restraints across my bare chest. I asked what was going on. The doctor plus a man and a woman I had never seen before came to tower over me. I think they were hungry—they barred their teeth. The doctor spoke in a low tone, indicating he did not truly want to speak with me. The others shook their heads with joy. The woman pointed at her head. Perhaps she wondered if I had a pain in my head. I said, "Din, din, din." They backed away. I had spoken loudly with respect so that even an elder could hear. She walked to a desk and brought back a photo of the Belatrin Bureau. Banners were hanging from its windows, with written characters on them. She pointed to the banners.

I understood. She thought that I spoke Belatrin, that for some reason a metamorphosis had occurred that had rewritten my mind. I remembered the Siirian's prediction that I might be the one to negotiate the treaty. It all made sense somehow—they had bypassed the Free Machines and sent in a device to reprogram my brain. A lower level bureaucrat would be perfect; we get our brains reprogrammed every day anyway. My friendly captors had reasoned this out, and wondered if I could read the banners. I may have the spoken language, but not the written one yet. I needed time and I wanted to find the Siirian

At least I thought that was what they were saying.

I tried to point to the restraints across my chest with

my chin. This produced no results. Then I tried to express my willingness to accept their commands by nodding my head up and down in the second gesture of submission.

This made them hungry again, but they released me.

I rotated my hands in a gesture of nudity. They seemed perplexed but the woman suddenly grasped what I was saying and my clothes were brought. I dressed and began walking slowly out of the Bureau. The doctor, the woman and the man and ten guards followed me. I walked down the dry dusty sweet-smelling street to the market.

The kiosk of the Siirian, who had sold me the air shield, lay empty. I jumped up and down to indicate this was the runaya, the hidden starting point that must be investigated if the event is to be known. I think my clear gesture was understood; the guards began talking to merchants on either side. One guard grabbed me gently. She treated me as thought I were an elder worthy of respect. I acknowledged her gesture and leaned on her arm. She was right. I was worthy of respect. I would end the war.

In many ways all of the fears of my life, of my generation and that of my parents and grandparents were melting away at this moment. I was the messiah. The nanlatoo.

As we walked back to the Bureau the guard kept a tight grasp on me. I was too precious to be loose.

At the Bureau they began brining me star maps. Some had sections colored in green, others in yellow, others in red. I knew this represented what I could give away, what was to be negotiated over and what must remain in human control I was hungry and showed my teeth often. Eventually they brought food.

I wished I could read star maps, but I was not worried. There would be time in the negotiations. Once I was in the in the picture the Free Machines would provide their services as go-betweens very cheaply.

The next morning they woke me up very early. They had the robes of a Duke of Diplomacy for me to wear. The pink sun had not risen, and few people were around. I ate a disgusting combination of fermented milk products by myself. Many people slapped my back, but I had done nothing wrong. At the end of the meal, they tied a ribbon around my brow. Our Eyez had seen the Belatrin wear such things. They sort of pushed me through the halls of the Bureau. I gathered there some sort of deadline. I didn't like the rough treatment. At the door they gave me the star maps and a several pages of instructions. I told them that these were of no help to me, but they just showed their teeth again.

Outside of the Bureau three land cars waited . They pushed me into the central one and sped off, I had never been outside of Humantown since planetfall. The pink sun was just rising, The weeping lavender trees and bright blue birds were lovely. I knew their names. They were inlaroo From time to time the trees caught one of the birds, but mainly they flew too swiftly. We drove for about thirty minutes when we came to a series of towers about ten meters high. The towers stood about ten meters apart. On our side of the towers was a thin bluish moss such as the ground cover of the forest, on the other side the earth had been scorched. I could see another set of towers in the distance.

We drove on.

When we stopped my driver handed me a pair of viewers. There was a round table set in the bare earth midway between the two rows of towers. It had two chairs. My driver took the viewers from me, and guards opened the door. I wanted music and song. I wanted to be recognized for my sacrifice.

They pulled me from the car

I dropped the star maps, but they gathered them up and gave them to me. They were bulky and hard to carry. I did not look like a nantaloo. The guards helped me up to the towers. One of them carried a small device which he clicked as we drew close. They shoved me toward the bare earth.

I did not want to go. I did not want to be their messiah. Let someone else end the war. I don't even know what our society would be like with no war. There had been war all my life, all my parent's life. I wanted to go back to my job. I wanted them to fix my brains.

One of the guards pulled a short rod from his belt and touched my arm with it. It shot burning pain. I whimpered. It was clear that I could not avoid this diplomatic mission. So I walked forward.

The bare earth beneath my feet felt like sandpaper. On the other side of the barrier I felt less afraid. Maybe

I was walking toward people that could understand me. I would guess the bare earth was about two kilometers in width. It took me less than ten minutes to walk to the table I pulled out a chair. I couldn't believe with the resources of two empires there wouldn't be at least a roof to sit under.

I watched the Belatrin side. Some small flying vehicles had landed and they were leaving them. A veiled figure, that I perceived to be a woman, began walking toward the barrier and then across the bare earth. I was wondering what lottery had chosen her, and if she were seen as a winner or a loser by her people.

It seemed to take a very long time for her to cross to me. She carried some silver scrolls. Her skin was light blue, her eyes dark green. I could not tell if she had hair. I realized that I was closer to a Belatrin than any human had ever been and not gone mad. She was closer to a human than any Belatrin had ever been and not died. At least as far as we know of.

When she approached, I stood up to pull out a chair for her. She seemed frightened by this action, and wouldn't sit until I returned to my side of the round table. She spread her scrolls out. They were covered in characters and diagrams that I didn't understand. So I stood and unrolled my star charts out over her scrolls.

"These are what we wish to agree to." I said.

Then she spoke.

Utter gibberish.

I wanted to garb her, shake her, slap her, scream at her. She must speak the language as I. My loss of a language, of a galaxy of friends and culture must mean something. She stared at the star maps and cried. She pushed my maps off the table and onto the dusty earth and began rolling up her scrolls.

I didn't understand her gesture, but not because of the curse of babel visited upon me. I simply didn't understand her purpose.

She stuffed the scrolls in the tubes and began walking past me toward the human side. She may have hypothesized that she had the human tongue I the Belatrin. Maybe it was a gift from the gods, or maybe it was a Free Machine sociology experiment.

I watched her go.

She walked slowly and deliberately, so they wouldn't shoot her. They showed great bravery and let her walk up to them. Then they rushed forward and hugged her. She must have had the key, the Word. Then they drew back and she convulsed. Whatever had changed her brain had not made her able to withstand humans. I could not tell if the humans were mad, or if they had been spared.

I thought about my options.

I gathered my star maps and began slowly walking toward the Belatrin. Maybe I will end the war.

Or maybe I'll just be a madman among people that understand what I am saying.

THE FLEEING

It was sixty years into the Belatrin war that humanity realized that the enemy was the Belatrin. At first the attacks were blamed on the Free Machines or the Siirians. Or perhaps some natural phenomena, that made men crazy or sick was at work. No one guessed that an active group was destroying the expansion of mankind, because none of the survivors gave coherent accounts. It wasn't established until recently what the circumstances of the first contact between mankind and the Belatrin had been. However when some of the log of *Vogt* was found in the Madeline Cluster (i.e. the furthest point away from Belatrin space), the name "Belatrin" entered usage. It was a good twenty years later before any human ships survived an encounter with a black cruiser.

The logs are problematical. Standard telemetry data is missing, as well as most of the formal logs of the crew. A great deal of effort had gone into bypassing the various safeguards of the recording system, apparently by Captain Rye (or perhaps Veda Scarab), motives are unclear, and a few experts have denounced the Vogt's logs as Belatrin propaganda. However, since no attempts at Belatrin propaganda are known of, others believe that the log is a legitimate human document. The philosophical speculations of Captain Rye can be dismissed as some form of mental strain and are included only for a sense of completeness.

The *Vogt* was not a ship of the Instrumentality. It was a Pleasure Class Exploration vehicle. In the years between the brief Siirian war and the declaration of war with the Belatrin, wealthy citizens were encouraged to buy and maintain small spacecraft for exploration purposes. The Instrumentality would provide a list of worlds know to be reasonably safe. These class M planets had no over-large predators, sentient life, terrible weather and so forth. The average spacecraft (and common sense) were all that were needed to engage in secondary planet surveys. The data collected was given over to the Instrumentality, and the survey party had various psychological benefits like being able to name planetary features. Occasionally the primary survey had missed the predator, or there were a class of virus not affected by the Benway Device, and such minor thrills provided amusement to the idle citizenry. It is hard for us to look back on that time without envy, but the Social Engineers assure that it is bad for us and the war effort to be envious of our own past. The ideal mindstate to absorb this data is to try and identify with the wealthy idle folks, who did these surveys. In the happy days after the war, we will be moving surplus populations to these worlds. You are advised to take class A or D mood enhancers now.

Failure to do so may a violation of the War Powers Act (Instrumentality Regs. 1-8895972-10-5).

FIRST ENTRY. After some static the scene clears, we see a pleasant woods, not unlike Earth of the distant past, except for the slightly purplish tinge of the foliage of the trees in the background. The five explorers are sitting at a circular table hovering a few centimeters off the slightly moving grass-like plants. Small chirrupy sounds are heard in the distance, perhaps a bird or insect analogue.

Captain Rye is in her late forties; her manner suggests that she once held office in the Instrumentality. Her gray eyes are relaxed. She knows she has chosen a safe and beautiful planet. William Scarab is thin and pale; probably just back from regeneration, maybe in his early hundreds. He looks bored and vaguely nauseous. Veda Scarab is in her early twenties, she looks like a minor vid-goddess, and in fact she is an expert on machine pseudo-psychology. Her eyes are bright pink and her teeth steel. She is very excited; no doubt this is her first time on a new world. Everett Jamieson is in his late fifties. His clothes suggest an African royal family, perhaps Nairobian Empire. He seems to be truly relaxed, the deep relaxation that only vast wealth can bring. Susan Chang is in her mid-sixties. She should probably have some kind of rejuvenation treatments soon. She seems a bit out of place, unaccustomed to the opulence that goes with the planetary exploration hobby.

"The communication/exploration satellites are in

place," said Rye. "I have to thank you again Mr. Scarab, for picking such a nice spot for planetfall."

"Well, I've been on these runs before, and I'm tired of the sort of thinking that said we have to pick out a polar region or a desert. Those will be inhabited eventually, but that's not our worry. I think this little area will have some nice vacation possibilities for a few decades. Did anyone of you float out to Scarab Falls yet? It makes the Victoria Falls on earth look paltry."

"How do they know this planet is safe?" asked Susan Chang. "I think we are too small minded about this."

"What do you mean?" asked Veda Scarab.

"Well, it could be that there is a sort of danger that we can't guess at yet." Said Chang.

"That's a meaningless argument," said William Scarab. "That could be said about walking along a corridor at home."

"No, I don't mean like slipping on a toy your child has dropped, but you hadn't seen. I mean something spiritual or psychological," continued Chang.

"Most forms of space madness are pretty well known," said Captain Rye.

"Why are you worried, Ms. Chang?" asked Jamieson.

"From the beginning of this trip I was worried," said Chang.

"If you don't mind my asking why are you on this trip," asked Jamison, "you don't seem to be well, the type."

"I spent my life savings on this trip—" begins Chang, and the log fades out at this point.

The next scene is aboard the *Vogt*. It is apparently recorded during breakfast. All are cheery and alert.

"I am having some problem with the sensors and recording devices." said Captain Rye. "One of the ship's Eyez said a small vehicle made planetfall last night, but other Eyez and Earz disagree. The unintelligent recording devices seem to be fading out as well. If I can't fix them, I will have to move our launch up to tomorrow. The Instrumentality demands our full records for the privilege of exploring."

"Exploring my ass." said William Scarab. "There's nothing we are doing that a dumb satellite couldn't do better."

"Except," said Susan Chang, "Testing psychological conditions."

"Paying money you mean," said William Scarab, "Oops, I guess that's a sore point with you."

"Anyway," said Captain Rye, "I want you and Mr. Jamieson to check out the location of the phantom planetfall." She points at Susan Chang.

Everyone soon leaves the galley. The recording tape rolls on for hours focused on the empty table. The next scene is abrupt. Rye looks angry, Susan Chang is weeping. The Scarabs are subdued.

"Why are you crying? What happened?" demanded Captain Rye.

"All I remember is walking into the clearing and we were looking at some tracks that had been made by a little machine. Two wheels about this far apart. I told Prince Jamieson that we should go get you at once. We had discovered that the radio wasn't working."

"I tested your radio when the Scarabs found you, it is working fine," said Captain Rye.

"He said that he was going to go ahead a little ways and see what was up. I was supposed to stay behind this big purple tree. I told him I was going to count to a hundred and that if he didn't come back I was coming to get you."

"This isn't god-damned hide-n-seek," said William Scarab.

"Tell me again what happened," said Captain Rye.

"I started counting, and then I was over by that lake and Veda was holding my hand," said Chang.

"Do you remember anything at all?" asked Captain Rye.

"No. Well yes. I sort of remember talking to Prince Jamieson later, and some running," said Chang.

"What did you talk with Jamieson about?"

"About leaving. He said he found something big and we should leave. He said he couldn't leave because he was part of it. He couldn't leave, but we should leave."

The Captain sent Chang off for medication, and continued her inquisition of the Scarabs.

"How did you find her?" she asked Veda Scarab.

"We were doing a life count on the river and the lake. William was under the surface of the water and I was sorting his data. The recorder wasn't working well and I was having to do it all by hand. when I heard her singing a song. I thought she had taken a little flyer up to see us, and was just being playful. She's a little weird you know, so I said 'Hello! Hello!' and then I saw she had this wild-eyed expression. I called William to the surface, and I led her to our flyer. She didn't fight with me or anything. William started searching for her flyer. We called you as soon as we realized that there was something deeply strange going on."

"You were unable to find the flyer?" asked Captain Rye. "You know he was a VIP, right? We're going to need to find him. I think he is playing a trick on Ms. Chang."

"No, Ma'am, I couldn't find the flyer, and the sensor log on our own showed no flyer activity. But the log gave out a few minutes after she showed up. Jamieson seemed like a nice type. He was taking the survey business seriously. I don't think he would scare Ms. Chang, but I tell you one thing. I am going to make trouble for your company when I get back, that woman is too unstable to be allowed to do this."

"I doubt if she was as forthcoming with the interviewers on Old Mars as she was with us the other day. I would like it if you and I could scope the area Jamieson disappeared in, if Mrs. Scarab doesn't mind staying in the ship. I will tell the ship to keep Ms. Chang sedated, but I would like someone here in case Jamieson flies back." Said Captain Rye.

"Why don't you call the flyer back?" asked William Scarab.

"Someone has bypassed my controls on the flyer they took out," said Captain Rye. "I want to know a little more before I yell for help. I've never yelled for help in anything I have ever done, and I was in the Second Division during the war."

"This is probably just a senescence failure. Sometimes the finer neural nets have cascading senescence—on e net drops and as the quality of the feed becomes both simpler and more random the next net actually convinces itself that is malfunctioning, not its feed. I wrote a few papers on Senescence Cascade in Free Machine politics when I was an exchange student." Said Veda Scarab, "If you can gave me high level access to the Vogt's systems I can root out the problem while you're gone. I disagree with my husband. I think it is goddamnned hide-n-seek. Jamison just got annoyed with her stories about her brother had disappeared and decided to ditch her. Her own problems created the rest."

"Maybe," said Captain Rye, "But did she get to your location without a flyer?"

"Oh she had a flyer," said Veda," Our equipment is just screwed up and didn't register it. I could be—"

The tape ends here. The next scene was a breathtakingly beautiful valley. The trees that line the valley are as large as Earth redwoods and are covered in a smooth dull purple skin. No animal noises of any kind can be heard. The recording probe was a little erratic focusing on Rye and Scarab, but occasionally making unordered close-ups of small pallid plants that resemble Earth mushrooms, or focusing on a small rock. Clearly the search had been going on for a while. Scarab and Rye look sweaty and tired; there is tension between them.

"Well, that must be the tracks," said Captain Rye. She points down at the ground. The probe must have been in failure mode, it did not follow her motion.

"They don't go anywhere. Just a few meters of wheel tracks," said Scarab.

"No Jamieson, and no phantom ship," said Rye.

"The flyer is fine," said Scarab.

"Yeah. I want you to fly that back," said Rye.

"If you don't mind, Ma'am, I would rather fly with you and set the flyer to automatic.," said Scarab.

The next scene is the galley. Veda Scarab has prepared a huge meal in the Chinese fashion. It looks like it could easily serve twelve. She has applied a chrome finish to her teeth and seems beside herself with glee.

"I found all of our problems. Something is interfering with net autonomy. It is as if each of the machines' nets is dissolving into a bigger whole, that wants to show us a different picture," said Veda Scarab.

"What kind of picture?" asked William.

"One we'd rather not see," said Veda, "Or perhaps simply cannot see. Or maybe only the best of us can see. It all makes me very hungry."

The last remark is delivered in a voice too high and shrill. Captain Rye excuses herself and goes off to check on Chang. Moments later, she runs back in the galley yelling that Chang is gone and wanting to know when and why and how. Veda seems absorbed in eating the moo shu pork and can't seem to grasp anything is wrong. Rye grabs some of the moo shu and runs off to the lab, clearly thinking that Susan Chang had become diner. William starts screaming at his wife, who merely giggles. The scene fades into static.

The next scene is in the galley. There is huge pile of cameras, recording crystals, Earz, and other telemetry devices. Captain Rye is examining each with the help of William Scarab.

"All they want to think about is Chinese cooking," said Rye. Her laugh is a little loud, momentarily sounding like Veda. Both notice the resemblance and she stops laughing. She continues, "I don't know what she did to these. Do you think she is trying to tell us what happened to Chang?"

"I don't care what happened to Chang. I want to leave," said William Scarab.

"Aren't you paying attention? The ship needs a certain number of Eyez and Earz to fly. I've got to get at least a third of these on-line, and your wife isn't exactly helpful."

"We've got to find out what happened to her," said William Scarab.

"What happened to her is that she went crazy, because there is something on this plant that the prelim survey didn't detect, and we will all go crazy if we don't leave."

"Is that your explanation then, that Jamison and Chang are crazy? So crazy that we can't find them?"

"No. I am worried that maybe you and I are crazy and just can't see them. Your wife is very insistent that Chang is still in her room. Who knows, maybe she's right."

The transition to the next scene takes longer. William Scarab and Captain Rye look tired and their clothes are drenched with sweat. It is hard to tell how much time has passed since the last scene. They are in the galley.

"We can't argue with her," said Captain Rye.

"We can force her," said William Scarab.

"I'm not going to force her," said Rye, "What was that word she came up with? Belephen?"

"*Belatrin*. She said the other ship is a Belatrin scout ship."

"There is no other ship, that was a sensor anomaly, a bad satellite."

"She is my wife. I am going to get her."

"I don't want you out there."

"What are you going to do—shoot me for picking up my wife?"

"I think she may be diseased. I think she have some contamination that made her do something to Chang."

William Scarab asked, "How can you think she did anything to Chang?"

"She was here. She is the only one that is smart enough to work over the devices. She is responsible. It's because she resents you. You bought the company she worked for. She told me."

"She worked for the Instrumentality. She's the one with the money. She paid for this trip, which includes your salary missy. I am going to get her."

"I may not let you back in the ship if you go down to that valley."

"There's nothing down there. There's just a couple of ruts in the ground and my wife."

"The sun's wrong down there. It's shifted. Look how bright it is in here."

"There's nothing wrong with the light in here."

The scene ends. The next scene is likewise in the galley; we can see through a porthole that the Vogt is in deep space. The Captain and William Rye are looking much better. They are in the confetti party clothes that were popular in the decades before the Belatrin war. The table is set for three.

Captain Rye said, "Tomorrow we will be able to take off, I have most of the Eyez and Earz on-line."

"Pity we have to go, Veda and I were just getting to like the planet. She had a great time with the other vacationers."

"Yes, I think it will be remembered as a great trip. I am thinking of taking last walk in the valley tonight as the moons rise. Maybe I'll even go skinny-dipping in the river."

"Isn't that a little loose with regulations?" asked Scarab.

"At the end of a voyage is time to unwind."

"You know it seemed for awhile there, that it was getting tense, but I can't remember why."

"Oh all trips are that way," said Captain Rye. "Then when you're over the willies, you forget why you were worried. When's your wife coming up to join us?"

"She's already here."

The scene ends. Veda Scarab was not there. The next

scene is on the bridge. Captain Rye is wearing a green Instrumentality cloak; William Scarab is dressed in vaguely military suit and cape. Both seem to making adjustments to the ship's course and speed, but as we look closer we see that the *Vogt* is on autopilot and that they carefully never actually touch any controls.

Captain Rye said, "I think we really understand about the Belatrin now."

"Yes," said Scarab, "We must report to the Instrumentality, Dame Administrator. I will prepare my reports in triplicate before tea."

"We are making good speed, mid-shipman."

For the next twenty minutes Captain Rye then calls off a checklist of nonsense terms like "Kundabuffer." To which Scarab said, "Check!"

In the last scene Captain Rye is alone on the bridge. She is still wearing her Instrumentality cape, but it has been decorated with bits of colored foil, which have been made to look like the medals for bravery, service, honor and so forth. She is addressing an unseen crowd.

"Ladies and gentlemen, the Vogt Expeditionary Force suffered great causalities during its undercover mission to infiltrate the Belatrin. Only General Beetle Scarab, and myself as you can see, survived. The many men, women and Free Machines that died on Planet Chang will not be forgotten. Our greatest discovery was that our ruthless and implacable enemies, the Belatrin, are so close to human beings in nature that we cannot stand them. Their reality is at odds with our own. They come from the other side of space. I am not talking here about the closed nature of the curved five-dimensional manifold that we think of space. I am talking here in a Belatrin concept. They are from the other side. They went too far and came out on the other side. It is only clear what this means when you have been with the Belatrin, fought with them against the horrors of their empire like the fanged ezwal. It is only clear when you have set with them during twelve course state dinners. It is only clear when you have made love to them under the mad racing moons of Jamieson II. There is, Sirs and Dames of the Instrumentality, only one thing to do. What we must do is Go. We must Go to the other side and beyond. We must go so far as to turn ourselves inside out, and then we will become the Belatrin. We will win by becoming the enemy, for you see we have already done so. They are us. Us from the other side, from the back of beyond. Only by being them can we conquer them. Otherwise, there is only madness."

She waits, apparently hearing applause, and then she takes a small device from her cloak. It may or may not be a hand-made laser of some sort. She points it at the recorder.

Then there is static.

For Willie Siros

A TALE FROM THE WAR

This happened in the last centuries of the Belatrin War to my grandfather.

On Lister IV there were a group of cybernetic engineers, who because of their connections with the Terran League, knew that their planet had been designated as a "strategic loss." Instead of dying as did so many other human patriots, they stole a small spacecraft and parked in orbit on the other side of the gas giant Lister VI. The great wavicle known as a mind-bomb engulfed Lister IV. Soon the twelve engineers found the craft to be small. For a year they cautiously maneuvered among the moons of the gas giant. On a frosty planetoid they found ruins of another star-faring civilization, and/or a season they practiced their arts trying to revive these ancient machines, but even this paled. For two long orbits of the ponderous planet they hid in the haunted moon as a vast Belatrin ship cruised the system. And their fear of the great black cruiser helped them pass the time. But the cruiser left and their frustration returned.

Some argued that they should attempt to contact the Terran League and accept the fate of a prison planet.

Others spoke of returning to Lister IV where they could fashion companions by their arts. Each could live several hundred kilometers from the others, and they would never have to see each other's stinking faces again.

But there had been the mind-bomb, and fragments of it might still be crawling along the magnetic fields of the planet. Above all, the engineers valued their minds. So fear and desire held them in stasis.

On the "day" they maneuvered their spacecraft into orbit around the seventh (and least interesting) moon, they came to a decision. The craft had a small one-man probe. They could send one of their number to Lister IV and if he or she survived, they would know it was safe to return. And if they perished—well at least it would be a little less crowded. So a program determined which among them—being sure to take neither the least nor the greatest of their craft—to send to Lister IV.

The lot fell upon my grandfather; and they stocked the probe with all manner of things he might need. As they stocked these things, they began to envy my grandfather. What if he found Lister IV clean of Belatrin mischief? What if the green hills of home proved so wonderful that he faked his demise?

They paused in their packing and held my grandfather in a small cell for three days. They considered torturing him for these crimes he might commit. After a long day with no food or drink, the craftiest of the engineers told him, "We have made a reading of your mind so precise that we can find it even if you download it from your brain into a machine. We can find it even if you put it in cold storage. If you have not returned to us by the northern winter solstice, we will send a sending against you. So strong will it be that any machine on the planet will seek you out and destroy you. Have a pleasant trip."

The onboard computers drove the probe. As he approached Lister IV, my grandfather saw the polar auroras in full flower. The remnants of the mind-bomb were still deteriorating, ionizing the air in sheets of cascading color. He had instructed the probe to make one equatorial and one polar orbit making full scans for sentient life, but he belayed that order. The sensors would never get through. So he picked Helka, a town of medium size, as his destination.

As the ship entered the atmosphere, his vision began to blur and he became very sleepy. The bulkheads of the probe began to melt and twist, and he saw a greater darkness beyond. The ship spread out, he slapped at the panel that disengaged all computer control. He tried to punch in a manual landing sequence on the spiny hide of afire-breathing cactus. His purple blood sang comic highlights from *The Marriage of Figaro*. In the lemon sky above, he saw a Belatrin cruiser descending. He tried to crawl through the smell of green ideas, but his tongue was too long and kept wrapping about vermilion brain coral. A locust whispered something in his ear and then he hurt very badly.

* * * * * * *

The probe had crashed into Robotic Police Station No. 5. When the effects of the mind-bomb largely passed, my grandfather found that the AI systems and their backups were hopelessly scrambled. The probe could be flown. If he got it away from the magneto-sphere of Lister IV the engineers could return him by remote control. The simple computers seemed alright and he released a hoard of mouse robots to effect minor repairs, forage for fuel, and effect perimeter scanning. He hoped that he was OK too. In the corners of his vision hair would grow or dark cats leap at him. Every few minutes he seemed to hear, "I'll kiss you later I'm eating a potato." Or he would sneeze uncontrollably.

The robot mice scurried over the surface of the probe, sounding like a gentle metal rain. Eating into the walls of the station they had managed to level the probe. Grandfather opened the door, and armed with only a few standard cyber-engineering tools, ventured out.

The town council of Helka in their whimsy had constructed its robot police in the form of giant chess pieces. These two- to three-meter tall figures lay throughout the green building. The walls and floors bore weapon burns. Driven mad by the mind-bomb they had slain countless hallucinatory enemies.

"Nov shmoz ka pop!" said a fallen knight.

The metal mice ate into their bodies seeking necessary circuits. Grandfather saw his first skeleton. He had never in his life seen a dead man—or any evidence of death. The very old always downloaded their minds.

But those archives would be gone too—save for the minds of the very rich, who could afford to have copies on other worlds. Death was considered a reasonable risk on frontier worlds. He sat with the skeleton for awhile trying to imagine what death could be like. Imagination dead imagine.

"Have the birds flown south for the winter?" said a door, and for an instant the world turned all manner of vivid pinks.

Outside there were smashed robots and smashed bones and smashed Sirian exoskeletons. It was a quiet world. Except for a few of the stupider pseudo-insects and the dumbest maintenance robots—nothing moved. With his tools, my grandfather was able to animate a small luxury land vehicle. While the mice prepared the probe for relaunch he explored.

He could cover three hundred kilometers a day. He dared not use his radio; although he was fairly sure that the mind-bomb was only active in the upper atmosphere—he didn't want to attract any fragments. Once he saw a great radio telescope, its unmoving bowl crawling with colored lights, still-living fragments of the mind-bomb. He drove nonstop for twelve hours to get away from it.

After a month he decided to return to the probe and fly back to Lister VI. Lister IV was inhabitable; although special shielding would be required to pass through the upper atmosphere. He theorized that if the probe made a high-speed launch at and perpendicular to the equator the limited exposure to the field would probably not damage his mind further. He seldom heard voices anymore. It had been five days since his car had said "Dull, empty, thud." He had—much to his surprise—grown lonely during the month. The voices in the stale air of the spacecraft seemed more desirable than the wind in the trees.

When first he saw the sunlight on her dark blue hair, he thought he was hallucinating. She stood tall and thin among the ruins of a theatre. She pulled pieces of tile off the fragment of wall. There was something of faerie about her and when she half-turned to put a particularly beautiful fragment of tile in her basket, grandfather was spellbound.

She saw him and grabbing up her tiny basket, gave a little cry.

He saw first her eyes darker blue than her hair, and then her fear. She was either real or alive or his mind had become totally unhinged. None of the hallucinations had lasted this long.

"Hello," he said. "Don't be afraid, I'm not here to steal your pretty things."

She put down her basket and walked slowly toward him. She putout her right hand and touched him just beneath his right eye. That warm and light touch meant more to him than anything before in his life, and his eyes began to tear. "You're alive," she said.

"I'm alive," he said. "Are you the only one left?"

* * * * * * *

She had made a home out of a small resort cottage.

She wasn't sure of what she had been or what she had done before the madness. She remembered the moon becoming blood and raining down on the forest of aluminum foil trees. She remembered talking to tall mushrooms and dancing with the stones. She remembered the pans and satyrs that came out of the living shadows and the strange games they had played. She remembered the talking statues and the white people with heads of rams who flew over her house or peered in her windows at night.

She had begun to build a wall around her cottage so that she would feel safe at night, when the aurora borealis turned the sky into a neon light show.

She wanted more than anything for my grandfather to stay. He wanted more than anything to stay. And it was two months to the Northern Solstice.

So he remained.

Each day when she went out to collect items for her wall, she wouldn't let him come along. She said that since he was going to leave her in a couple of months, she didn't want anything to remind her of him. If he was going to be so cruel as to leave her.

He protested that it wasn't cruelty. Just self-preservation.

She brought back interesting things for her wall bright green copper-bearing rocks, ornamental tile, human skulls, robot arms, fragments of sculpture, Siirian claws, rock crystal, melted metal sandglass. The wall sparkled in the sun. Moss grew on claw and skull. There was something crazy about the wall. Something in the sum of its parts that pointed in a direction that his mind couldn't go or wouldn't go. Something half remembered or glimpsed in a dream. The wall stood to her waist. She'd already found a massive iron gate. He couldn't imagine how she had carried it and installed it.

He offered to animate some robots for her. She declined.

But otherwise they were happy. They read to one another—or tended her garden—or scavenged delicacies from the finest homes of the city. They rode to the museums, to the canyons, to Siirian sonic sculpture gardens. They sang together. They made love, and my grandfather came to the realization that this was the happiest he'd ever been—ever could be.

He told her that he would return to her after he reported to the engineers. She said he would never return, and that she would spend the rest of her days thinking that he had been a sweet dream in her life of nightmare. "Besides," she asked, "What could happen?"

"The engineers would create a great self-sustaining wavicle. It would pass through space drawing energy into its structure much as an amoeba draws food into itself. It would seek me out—because it knows exactly what my energy tastes like. And then it would animate the robots—spot welding broken wires—punching through connectors—and the machine will become a monstrous engine of annihilation."

"Like what the Belatrin sent?"

"The opposite. Their sending increased entropy, ours is negentropic. Ours is a life-form. Theirs for lack of a better word is a death-form. That is why we fear the Belatrin so much. We fear they may be like their weapons."

"Your weapon brings death."

"It brings death through its own life like the pseudo-tigers in the hills."

"Or like men. Men bring death through their life."

"Or like men."

* * * * * *

In the sixth week of his stay, my grandfather had two more surprises. The first was seeing her open her stomach. They had had a wonderful meal of ssarinst, the only Siirian food he found tasty. She had said she needed a walk, and he decided to catch up with her as a lover's game. He tracked her quietly through the woods.

She sat on a stump and by drawing a line with her index finger opened her stomach. She removed a bag full of food, dumped out three quarters of it, and replaced it.

He realized that she must have been a very expensive pleasure robot. She would only need a little food for her organic parts. Probably one that a rich executive kept stashed deep underground—took it out for holidays or traveling. The shielding must have saved it—only disrupting the stasis field that kept it—no, kept her, he decided—fresh. He realized that he loved her, and if she wanted her secret kept, it would be kept. He walked away very quietly. He would never follow her again.

The second surprise is a surprise to husbands everywhere. She was pregnant. He knew that the more expensive models had this capacity. It was the ultimate egoboost—the robot created a DNAless egg and took the chromosomes from the semen to create a full set of chromosomes. The robot, which had observed and analyzed the personality of her master, would recreate that personality in the child. She said that since he was going—she would make sure she wasn't alone.

When the wall was as high as her head the first feathery flakes of snow fell. My grandfather looked out that morning and suddenly realized that he had lost track of time. He asked her what day it was; and she smiled, and told him, it was two days before winter solstice.

He ran for his car, but she stopped him. He could never make it back to the moons of Lister VI in two days. If he was going to die—wouldn't he want to die with her? He saw her reasoning and went in to stoke the fire.

"Besides," she said, "A love like ours is a rare thing and I think I may be able to stop their sending."

The day of the Solstice came, and he lived; but when night came he became very drowsy. The sending was interacting with his energies. He would fall in and out of sleep. She became busy. She knocked down a section of her wall. She was much, much stronger than he had guessed. She found a glittery black something. She seemed to be talking to it.

Around eight in the evening the parade of broken robots began to make its way from town. Some hopped on one leg. Others lurched along on three. One of the police robots, a black knight, who glided on electromagnetic waves of force; led the procession. My grandfather watched the sky, because he felt too weak to run or fight. He saw that for the first time the sky was clear of Belatrin aurora.

My grandmother, for as many of you have guessed it was she, stood her ground in the broken section of wall. She warned the damaged machines that this was her home, and that they should turn back. But the machines marched for only one purpose.

When they had come within four meters, the police robot tried to fire on her. But its faulty control merely took out more of the wall.

My grandmother lobbed the black crystal into their midst. For an instant nothing happened, then a corona discharge limned the robots. The floating knight fell and the others stopped moving. Then it was dark and as grandfather lost consciousness, he saw her begin rebuilding her wall.

It snowed a lot in the winter and grandmother's belly began to swell. Grandfather told her that he must return by the spring equinox, because the engineers would try again. They would practice their dark craft until they were able to overcome her secrets.

So again they played the long game of her coy love.

She convinced him that the people in their tiny ship were not of the forgive and forget variety. As soon as they knew for sure that Lister IV was safe, he was a dead man. If he radioed to them, they would seek him out. And certainly they would kill him the instant his ship was seen by their electronic eyes. Just as he had lived for love, he must trust her love for him to live.

He asked where she had learned arts that were beyond his engineering. She said that if he knew, he would know fear. He remembered the stale air of the small ship during the months they had watched the Belatrin cruiser. So he never asked.

Flowers of every color and form bloomed, and the flowering pseudo-grass of Lister IV put forth its tiny saffron florets. Everything was in life save for my grandfather's mind which was in the midst of death.

"I have calculated," my grandmother said, "That I may not be able to stop the next sending of the engineers. We will have to have help. Come with me."

My grandmother now big with child led him to one of the largest houses in the nearby city. It had been made in the neoclassical Terran style, with red brick and white-painted columns. The security system of the house was up and running. A brief heat passed over my grandfather as he walked toward the gate; two Grecian statues turned toward him. He guessed there were lasers within their eyes. The gate swung open.

"How does this work?" he asked. "Why is any of this up?"

"I don't know," she said. "It wasn't this way before."

The front door opened and a headless butler robot showed them the most opulence that a frontier planet could manage. Through the kitchen, down to a wine cellar, through a secret door to an elevator. Then down. Deep.

Beyond the elevator door lay a pleasure garden to end pleasure gardens. Fountains of wine, beautiful birds in jeweled cages, deep living carpets of nesstra, gentle harp music. My grandfather guessed that her master must have survived and re-begun his paradise.

Then she passed beyond an ebon column. On the other side the smooth marble wall was broken by an angry vent. She went into the darkness beyond. He activated a small hand light, but she struck it from his hand.

The walls of the cave were made of a dark crystalline material. He recognized it. Not only as the weapon she'd employed, but also as the ancient machinery he'd helped examine on a moon of Lister VI.

Something in the cave spoke, "Foster daughter, I see you are with child."

"Yes I am and I have come to ask a favor for him."

"Foster daughter, it must be a fearsome thing that you are come here. Tell me what you wish."

She told him the whole story.

"I can save the father of my grandchild. Go and do not disturb me further."

Spring equinox came. My grandmother put my grandfather on a chair in the beautiful garden around her foster father's house. The headless butler served tea and watercress sandwiches. There was a little warmth in the air, and grandfather was beginning to think that perhaps he'd survive this as well. Near ten in the evening a green star appeared in the heavens. This was a much more powerful sending.

The green light slowly fell through the sky—growing brighter and bigger as it descended. My grandfather wanted to run, but grandmother put her hand on his chest so he couldn't move.

"I'll die," he said.

"You will not die, father of my grandchild, be still and do not disturb my concentration," said the voice.

My grandfather thought of the descending teardrop of light as a terrible acid to eat his bones. He expected the headless butler to bash his head with the heavy silver tray.

The teardrop seemed to strike an invisible dome above the mansion. By now it shone as bright as twenty suns, and my grandfather feared that he would go blind even through his closed lids. A cool hand shielded his face, and he remembered his love and why he was here.

The teardrop of light began to roll down the invisible dome. When it hit the ground, it sped off like quicksilver. My grandmother released my grandfather's face.

"It's over," he sighed.

"No," said the voice, "its just beginning."

My grandmother continued to hold him down. When he started to speak she put her hand over his mouth. For an hour she held him and all they could hear was the pseudo-birds.

Then there was a rumbling of machinery. The black queen, bishops, rooks, and pawns floated toward the mansion grounds. As they approached, the gate opened. Grandfather waited for the lasers to melt the floating parade. But they floated into the grounds. The headless butler rolled in front of them and led them down the walk. The front door of the house opened and they floated in.

It was a long parade of doormen, security workers, longshoremen, teachers, and robots grandfather couldn't identify. Some would step off the trail and move toward my grandfather's chair. The butler would wheel over and gently push them back.

After the last robot entered, things were again quiet. But my grandmother continued to pin him. Smoke began to drift out of the front door. A little at first. Then a lot.

The voice said, "It is ended. Go."

* * * * * * *

In late spring my father was born. It goes without saying that he had granddad's eyes, nose, and so forth.

My grandfather hated my father. He had had grandmother all to himself. He began exploring the ruins again. One day as he explored the shadows of a great laboratory, chance toppled a robot scientist. When the machine clattered to the floor its noise filled him with fear. My grandfather's heart beat so loudly that he imagined they could hear on Lister VI. He had thought that a sending had found him. Now he knew he was a coward. He had risked nothing to gain his brief paradise. Now when something even more helpless than he had come along he had lost it. My grandfather cried among the ruins. Nothing in his life had prepared him for the testing of life. He had been a wizard among wizards and he was as far from humanity as those fools floating around the cold moons. When his crying passed, he decided to run to grandmother, because that is the way we are. Once we discover a secret about ourselves we must find someone, even our worst enemy to tell it to. Where this commandment comes from I do not know.

Unfortunately pleasure robots aren't programmed to understand cowardice. They are meant to raise executives after all. They seek to weed out the evil of their owners. In this they reflect a very deep fantasy of their designers. But she listened (and at my request played back the conversation years later).

She told him that her foster father wanted to see his grandson. So she would take the child to the dark cave for the afternoon, and my grandfather briefly regained what he had lost.

Then one day she came back and said that her foster father had detected that the engineers were preparing an all-out sending for the summer solstice. He had said that the child's energies were so like his father's that he might be in danger. He would be safe in the cave.

My grandfather had no fear of the sending. Had they not stopped the last two? He made a great show of bravado as though he had had anything to do with his own protection.

The night of the summer solstice came and my grand-father lay in a double hammock he'd made behind his cottage. Eight passed and all was well. When it was near midnight he decided that the engineers had been thwarted by his father-in-law. He called grandmother to him.

"We've beaten them," he said.

"Why do you think so?" she asked.

"Soon it will be tomorrow and their sending hasn't come," he said.

"Of course it came, it came at noon the sunlight hiding its approach."

"How do you know?"

"The people you abandoned are greatly filled of hate so they designed an awful fate for you. The sending found the robot closest to you." And she hugged him to death.

From my father's genetic material came the physical heritage of the new people of Lister IV. From the one in the cave came our psychic heritage, and this blend gave us the elements we needed for the role we were to play in the history of the galaxy.

MARS 1, BURROUGHS 2

The Heat was closing in. William Seward Burroughs hadn't felt that feeling since his resurrection in the early twenty-second century, but you can always smell some do-gooding son-of-a-bitch. Even if you are the living dead secure in bunker deep beneath the Chryse Plain of Mars. Somebody or Something wanted him, or perhaps just one of the dead men of Mars. He suspected the Belatrin or their allies. But everyone suspected them. The way to deal with such unwanted intrusions is to meet them with a form of physic jujitsu. Grab their reaching tentacle and pull it closer to you. Cold dead crab eyes scanned the inside of the basalt-walled bunker, time to go.

The ceiling unscrewed and he stepped out onto the red-brown plain. It stretched as far as was painful. A dry mummy-like shape emerged. It rose and tested the wind—a balmy -7 degrees C. and 250 kilometers an hour. Ah, Northern Hemisphere spring. Burroughs smelled something foul, something wormy. He allowed energy to flicker into the dim precog centers of his brain for the first time in years. Something oppressive was coming from Aldebaran clearly visible in the noonday sun. Mars was better for precognition than Earth, the magnetic field had waned with the ending of the plate tectonic billions of years before. Burroughs tapped a remote control. The Sojourner rolled up. He had souped-up that old piece of NASA junk when he arrived here in 2317. He sat on the old recliner stolen from the trash midden of Bradbury City and headed off to Humansville.

For the last eighty Martian years Burroughs had studied a vessel—the human vessel. When humans figured out the Belatrin vessel was the same vessel, used by a different type of the Nova Mob, nameless assholes, folks became interested in Bill. Millennia ago a stranded space traveler needed the human vessel to continue his journey and s/he/it made it for that purpose. Maybe the traveler died before he could use it. Maybe he used it and left the set. The human artifact has no more meaning than an arrowhead left in the dust. But Burroughs was learning the why and where-fores of that arrow in the hands of a master archer. The human artifact was the creator's last card played in a terrifying game years ago. The creator knew how to really travel—none of this spaceship travel at near light speed. At that speed you'd never get a chance to go anywhere. He would follow the creator outward.

At Weinbuamgrad Burroughs slit the plastic wall of the dome with his athame and stepped in. The self-sealing polymer closed behind him without a scar. Burroughs muttered a short locator spell and sniffed the air. He headed for the Green Brain.

Weinbaumgrad was a typical Martian town. That is to say, boring. It had three industries—mining, metallurgy, and entertainment to keep the miners and the metalsmiths from going crazy. This last industry had both legal and illegal manifestations. The Green Brain floated between the two. With hesitation Burroughs plunged into the manstorm. He pushed his way through vendors of expert elixirs, who for a few golden toels offered the miners the chance to be a concert pianist or a brain surgeon for a few hours. He passed gladiator joints where miners could fight each other or giant scorpions. Finally he felt that aura of seediness, which had not changed since his last visit forty years ago, and he knew this must be the Green Brain. He crossed the metal slidewalk, carefully walking into the middle of a licensed domestic murder.

Kyle Chiang drew a bead on the Deliah Xorn's back. That little slut wasn't gonna run around on him. He blew her a kiss and pulled the trigger. At that moment Burroughs stepped into the dart's path. It pierced his dead flesh and injected its manta ray poison into the dead optic nerve of Burroughs's right eye. Burroughs pulled on the dart. It snagged on his skull but finally popped out. He arranged his hair over the hole, snapped the dart in two, and walked in. Burroughs ordered a cohaba snuff. He put the forked stick to his new nose and snorted. His flesh swooned as he got direct sensory input from his dead core. The room grew sharp. Collapse the wave function and you kill Schrödinger's kitty He ordered a double Sahara martini and took a small table near the door.

He looked like a saint or a con man with his gray flesh and white desert robes. Kyle Chiang came into the bar looking for his kill. Killing a stranger unprovoked meant a huge fine and Kyle was a law-abiding man. He took one look at Burroughs and fainted dead away

Burroughs sprang up and caught Kyle as he fell. He quickly intoned the twelve-syllable call from the Typhonian Tablet. One of his familiar spirits inhabited Kyle's body. To the onlookers, the two men seemed locked in a passionate embrace. Burroughs released him.

(Vaudeville with limelight.)

"Kyle" spoke first.

"Well, Bill, how you eating?"

"Tol'able, K.C. Tol'able."

They sat.

"I haven't seen you since we ran skins at Venusport."

"Those were the days." Burroughs signaled for drinks.

"What brings you Mars way?"

"Thought I'd cool my heels and look up a few old friends."

"You on the run, Bill?"

"A man's always on the run if he's alive," Burroughs chuckled, "And it was such a pretty scam, too. Hassan's Ethical Used Slave Lot. The Octave Doctor ran the biology side and I was Public Relations. Of course we weren't catching the slaves like the law sez you should.

We'd bought a People's Republic Long Pork Tank and gimmicked it to put out the whole clone. We'd gather a few cells from our customers when they put their fingers on the credit grid."

"Sounds great. What went wrong?"

"The O.D. ran up a bunch of Sultans of Belize. Trouble is the original Sultan paid an unexpected call and thought he'd wandered into a Hall of Mirrors. The O.D. was customizing 'em with scars and tattoos. Turns out neither the Sultan nor his commandos have a sense of humor at all. I heard about it at the Gibraltar spaceport and the rest as the cliché runs is history. But tell me, son, how you're keeping yourself?"

The ventriloquism routine lasted long into the Martian night. Burroughs knew it was successful when the blackjack crashed into his skull as he stepped onto the metal slidewalk.

Dead eyes opened. He lay at one of the foci of an oval room covered in a smart plastic the deep deep yellow of a decayed tooth. There were no doors. At the other foci stood a rough crusty mauve Swiss cheese of a column—maybe two meters tall. From one of the holes near its base a black-segmented worm oozed forth. The five-centimeter diameter worm came from a three-centimeter diameter column. When it had stretched twenty centimeters from the hole short black erectile hairs broke through the chitin. A thin green slime began to drip from each hair onto the plastic floor. The black worm gism smelled of sauerkraut and mashed shield bugs. Burroughs decided this must be an Aldebarian, a creature, which need never fear social acceptance. They had shown up shortly after the Free Machines had contacted mankind, Burroughs had read about them, but having one wriggling in front of him was a new way of knowing.

<< we have examined your identification you are Yen Lee a notorious member of the Terran underworld please do not feign ignorance as your companion Kyle Chiang did we had to feed him to a ganymedian fungusdog we have an interesting proposition for you we will offer one thousand gold toels for a minor service refuse and we will kill you in an unpleasant manner >>

Burroughs had experienced telepathy before, but never a form, which so strongly tempted the gag reflex. He thought briefly of the piles of gold at his house— when he'd first discovered the Stone he couldn't make enough of it.

Burroughs spoke, "It doesn't seem to be much of a choice. What's the caper?"

<< we wish you to addict the population to di-oxy-hydro-heroin >>

"You didn't come six years by subspace drive to set up a junk empire." Six years, Burroughs thought, what a stupid way to travel. Don't these worms have any ambition? They were as bad as *Homo sapiens* or maybe *Homo sapiens* was as bad as Them. An image of the Mayan Centipede Cult flashed in his dead brain. The young brown men forced into the copper centipede before being roasted alive. Beginning of calendars.

Word falling. Image falling. "Let's do our William Tell act."

<< we want to gain mining rights we will demonstrate that humans can't take the boredom of mars by pointing out the drug dependency rate to the U N council >>

"What do you need me for? Di-ox establishes dependency after one shot. You could dump it in the water supply and sell the stuff on the slideways.. Shit people would wade through waist deep sewage and big to buy a shot from you. Simple algebra of need. Besides Martian governments are bound by the council anymore. At least in theory."

<< we MUST not be connected with the operation The Martian governments will fall. We have experience getting humans to work for us >>

"So you need me to your Palmer Eldritch? Your Dr. Benway? Where's the junk?" asked Burroughs.

<< we have several liters in one of our labs you will compound it into ampoules tablets and suppositories in the proportions your previous experience has indicated >>

"How do I pick up my gold?"

<< after you've established a need you will radio your contacts on earth to send more di-ox we trust the terran underworld to continue your fine work after Weinbaumgrad falls the triad will naturally expand to other Martian markets we will sit idly by bemoaning the fate of the Martian mines we'll monitor your first broadcast to earth and if we are satisfied we will supply

the location of a clarke subsystem flier in which the gold has been cached >>

"How can I trust you?" It was a ritual question, you couldn't trust any fink, but language demands we say certain things at certain times. Language is a virus.

<< you have no doubt that we will kill you why doubt we will pay you >>

Burroughs simply couldn't allow the worms in. It would ruin his base and plans. Now when he was so close to understanding the uses of the human vessel. It had been his goal even back at Harvard. When the Octave Doctor had resurrected him, his first words were, "I'll be back in No Time."

"I'll do it." Burroughs let out a long sigh oddly sibilant. Ninety-three kilometers away, a black basalt stone sculpture of a vulture opened its eyes. The vulture was Mut, the Egyptian symbol of motherhood. Good mommas vomit up dead things to their mewling infants.

<< a wise decision, Mr. Lee, this interview is at a close >>

To Burroughs's disgusted surprise, a D-shaped section of the floor canted under him, spilling him like so much garbage onto a lower level. A many-armed machine grabbed him and cut an incision in his left shoulder. A machine arm thrust a tiny pellet within. The arms closed the wound; another placed a slip of paper in a robe pocket. During the whole process he had been descending. He slid out a chute onto the trash midden where nanocytes munched on shit-stained comics and used condoms. He pulled himself out of the noisome muck like a lungfish crawling out of a puddle.

As the slideway carried him away he stared at the strange ebony angles of Aldebarian Legation in the two-moon night. They were scavengers, Burroughs thought, used the human vessel after the master had moved on. Mining a planet, a real race should be getting power from a magnetar. These soulless cretins probably used dead novas to brew control drugs. Spineless assholes.

The lab lay beneath A. J. Fooditorium, the most popular joint in Weinbaumgrad. On the west wall a giant black phallus pissed Champaign, chicken broth, martinis, Alexanders, coffees, hibiscus mint tea, mother's milk, diet root beer, Slusho, moonshine and grog into a ten meter long trough marked DRINKS. On the easy wall a rubber sphincter pooped baked Alaskan, chocolate-covered bacon, eggs benedict, fillet mingons, crawfish jambalaya, roasted Portobello mushrooms, cheeseburgers, fatty tuna, bagels with lox, and beef Wellington into a similar trough marked EATS. A.J. sprayed the room with a mixture of Cynarin and hunger-triggering pheromones. The smell of vomit rose in clouds, as well as seeped downwards into the drug lab.

Burroughs checked the room carefully for monitoring devices. He found none; he wasn't expecting any. The shoulder device should be enough. He cleared the table and lay upon it. He crossed his hands over this chest and hummed a song that was old when the pyramids were new. He sent his vision into his body and examined the pellet, a simple bomb triggered by an EPR bridge. They could probably just think him to explode, as an old exterminator he could see the beauty of thing.

He opened the plastic bottles of di-ox and poured them one by one into the sink. He set the ampoule machine, the suppository machine, and the tablet machine. He drew up the lab's only chair and sat facing the tiny window near the ceiling of the lab.

He waited.

He reminisced about the night he came forth. His grave stood near the old man's Egyptian obelisk. William S. Burroughs I, the inventor of a very useable adding machine. The Octave Doctor had drawn a circle around his grave with some phosphorescent metal paste. The OD sang a Naacal hymn to the tune of "East St. Louis Toodle-oo." The names of powerful daemons were written around the circle: Bradley-Martin, Erbeth, Nyarlathotep, Uranium Kid, Ah Pook, Pharol.

The Octave Doctor asked, "What is your Name?"

"I Will be back in No Time."

Their partnership worked well. Burroughs had his uncle Ivy Lee's flair for public relations. "'Poison Ivy' they used to call him. He made people love the Rockefellers."

Burroughs had tried to explain to the Octave Doctor about the human artifact.

"Think of it this way, O.D. When the first fish grew

lungs it wasn't trying to breathe air. It was trying to survive a wiggle over to the next pond. But once it had lungs it was stuck with them. See? It had tried to get to water and that stuck it in air. You can't go back. Whales didn't get gills back when they went into the water. Humans want to go into Space because the need Time. They want to outsource our problems to space. Throw our trash into the sun. Mine Mars and the Kuiper Belt, but maybe that search for more time will give us Space, like air for the lungfish."

The Octave Doctor asked, "Why do you care, Bill?"

"It's a family obsession. My ancestor William H. Seward bought Alaska for the US at two cents on the acre. He had the right idea OD, get the space. We are Here To Go. It's all about *lebensraum*, baby."

Burroughs waited for two hours. Just before the Martian dawn something scratched the window. Burroughs opened it and the black basalt vulture flew in on ponderous wings. It could have never managed earth gravity. Mut vomited a sparkly green powder into a stainless steel cauldron. It looked like crushed Christmas ornaments form Bill's Midwestern past, a glittery four-hundred-year-old nostalgia. Burroughs impatiently signaled for the neter to depart the vulture was well perched and the statue fell from the lab table breaking into myriad pieces. Flecks of olivine and feldspar glistened under the LED light.

Burroughs began sifting his dead fingers through the strange alkaloid, while he called upon the God of Pain and Music, the Goddess of the Zoneless Ones, and the God Whose Image is Found on Asteroids. Soon a gray humming filled the room and the mixture began to effervesce a color not found in this part of space-time. Burroughs removed his right eye and poured the mixture of marine ray poison and mummified brain into the bowl. That should give it the right kick. He replaced the sticky remains of his eye and began pouring the resulting mixture into the three machines. Towards noon he went upstairs and asked to borrow a pepper mill. While when the busboy went for it, he flung a handful of the powder into EATS.

Downstairs the God Whose Image is Found on Asteroids had sent the Red Mist. Burroughs gave It his wishes....

At the spaceport a furtive seedy old man in a faded rose trench coat approached a cadet, "Hey kid, want to see the stars?" an unwashed hand offering pills...a brightly burnished copper robot replaced the suppositories in the cold locker at Weinbaumgrad General Hospital and then began to inject something into the IV bags...a sharp-featured woman in a scarlet coat joined the ranks of expert elixir vendors...the ruddy-faced barman at the Space Rat said, "Hey, Mac, you just gotta try this new drink I just invented. I call it Midnight Surprise"...at the Vermilion Rose Tattoo Shop "Red" laughed as he fills up his dye needles...the new girl wearing the firetruck red gown of the technical class began her day by changing the liquid in the filter masks worn by people who must work outside the dome...Ruby made a new icing for the ever popular cinnamon rolls at the Sweet Tooth...pink-haired old women sold roses for the space dead at Rogoz Square, "Don't they smell sweet, sir?"...a crimson-capped postrobot put new stamps in the vending machines and destroys the old...a blushing priest officiated his first Mass at St. John the Divine, "The Blood of Christ," "Amen"...a scarlet claw materialized centimeters above the main holding tank of Weinbaumgrad's water supply and poured a vial of unknown liquid into the placid water....

Four Aldebarian androids, shaped like American lawn jockeys, captured Burroughs just at sundown. He was making a slow getaway on the Soujouner and was still in sight of the dome.

They imprison him in a windowless gray room. Burroughs shrugs. Didn't Hassan i Sabbah the Old Man break through in the Gray Room? And he lived in the year one thousand. The wall dissolved. The mauve column stood in the center of another gray room. The worm writhed out. Its thoughts were jagged as ground glass against Burroughs' artistic psyche.

<< you failed us >>

"Then why didn't you kill me?" Burroughs asked indifferently.

<< we were curious why did you distribute a different drug why a hallucinogen why such large-scale distri-bution?? you have nothing to gain >>

Burroughs shrugged. Another wall dissolved revealing a bank of monitors. Various scenes were revealed throughout Weinbaumgrad. If only Poison

Ivy's gift of gab wouldn't fail him now.

"You spineless assholes got nothing on me. You wanted 'em drugged, they're drugged."

<< but with what and why?? >>

"It is a little potion I made up years ago. It is based on the drug Hassan I. Sabbah used to give his assassins to see Paradise. I call it N-5D- dimyltryptamine. It is related to yage, a drug I tried centuries ago on Earth. I took the active ingredient a lovely little alkaloid called DMT, and I put a five-dimensional kink in its indole ring."

<< we do not think you can have multi-dimensional chemistry. We are confused. What have you done?? >>

The scenes were melting on the monitors. The sterile conapts of Sector Nine were turning into cylinder houses that could be raised on poles to escape assassination attempts. A black woman walking her white poodle began to change. Her skin became red, her clothes changed into a jeweled leather harness. Her dog's hair smoked off and he began growing in size and adding legs. Its head morphed into something like a frog, and it began trotting on ten short legs. It sprouted three sharp tusks. It was easily the size of an Earth pony. The Nitey-Night bedding shop wavered like light on a dying soap bubble and refocused as Gur Tus Sleeping Furs, then those letters changed into something exotic, unearthly.

"You see when ever the maker of the human vessels made it, it had to incorporate both time-binding and imagination. I know you worms have no imagination, so you will have a hard time working this into your seven lobed brains. Human consciousness is like a quantum consistent history. Murray Gell-Man figured that out almost four hundred years ago. You can make several readings of an electron, but you can only read either location or momentum at the same time. The electron behaves as though it were in all of the places and speeds because of collapse of the wave function seen as aggregate data."

<< what have you done?? We will activate the bomb in you. Do not lecture us on human understanding of quantum physics. Will your drug destroy the miners? >>

"Keep your cilia on, Gertrude! As I was saying humans spend a lot of their time in an unknown zone, and only when the real world collapses...."

Meanwhile the Church of St. John the Divine was opening its door after Mass. A wave ran through the neo-Soviet cathedral. Its pre-stressed concrete beams became frescoed scenes of the Tree of Life in the Valley of Dor. Its steeple was now a golden jewel encrusted spire. The words above the door change from the sixteen verse of the third chapter of John into" Great Is The Goddess Issus Who Rules the Paradise Of The Holy Therns" and then these words change into the strange script. The elderly mother of the bride has become a thousand year old red woman, "By the mother of the further moon, I think your wedding was as fine as any jeddara!"

"These flashes of imposed measurement let the

human vessel fold its form. The other moments are random. Day-dreaming we call it."

<< what is happening?? Will this destroy the miners?? >>

"The miners? Oh yes. The miners. My family has never much cared for miners Why my uncle Ivy Ledbetter Lee. That's where I took my street name of Yen Lee, don'cha see? He covered up the Ludlow Massacre, Colorado coal mining riot for John D. Rockefeller. Bloody business that twenty dead. Eleven of them children. No I am not pro-miner. You can bet your glistening little black body on that. I think I know you guys, there was a centipede worship cult in Mexico, I was studying that when I was there. I think your people might have visited our people once. Mighty strange co-incidence. The Ugly Spirit attached itself to me when I lived in Mexico City. I spent all my life trying to write it out, sort of a psychic diarrhea. Did you leave it there?"

The remote camera on the Western side of the dome showed that Earth had risen, a sapphire blue star. The dome shimmered and vanished. Burroughs' tricked-out Sojourner began to vibrate into a new shape, a vast living beast it must have stood three meters at the shoulder. It had four legs on either side, and lashed a broad flat tail. It was entirely devoid of hair, but was of a dark slate color and exceedingly smooth and glossy. Its belly was white, and its legs shaded from the slate of its shoulders and hips to a vivid yellow at the feet. The salvaged recliner became a great leather saddle decorated in the style of Thark. The throat no longer stood on the rocky brown-red soil but upon soft ochre colored moss that stretched as far as the camera could see. Then the screen went blank, as had many other monitors.

"You see," continued Burroughs, "The day-dreaming could be a key. What if consciousness would only check a certain pattern that was a different reality? A universe next door, perhaps, untouched by the Ugly Spirit your people left. Money and Progress and certain aspects of the language virus—what if we didn't need to buy your junk anymore? Mining rights on planets? Feh, you are worms. Little bits of throbbing gristle"

The voice of the Aledebrian's seemed faint and staticy.

<< What have you done?? What is happening?? >>

"The human vessel is Here To Go. I just gave it a new drug different than the language virus drug you brewed in some dead nova. My expert elixir is Burroughszine. Mars is no more. You are looking at Barsoom, I first read *Gods of Mars* at the Los Alamos Ranch School. Mr. Edgar Rice Burroughs was (sadly) no relation, but he showed me how religion and so forth could be control systems. After that I always wanted a Barsoomian Radium Rifle, the shells explode in sunlight don'cha know? I loved all of them: *The Chessmen of Mars*, *Synthetic Men of Mars*, "Skeleton Men of Jupiter."

On the last screen two men were running out of

A.J. Fooditorium. Their existential panic vanished, as they morphed into tall four-armed green men— olive skinned, hairless, protruding and independently working eyes, antenna like ears, tusks. They were magnificent! Easily four meters tall. One pulled a sword on the other, "You son of a calot! I will send you to your ancestors!"

The screen flicked out.

The worm voice was far and thin

<< the bomb. We will kill. >>

It dissolved into static. The building grew unsub- stantial. The bomb blew up in the black worm's reality tunnel. Like any good artist William S. Burroughs had melted into his art.

He noted that he was no longer a dead man, but an aged Barsoomian with a large cranium and multi- lensed glasses and a hearing aide. Hmm, the city had been Weinbaumrgad had become modern—there were one man equilibrimotors, shadowless street lights and a foul marshy smell. Ah, it must be Toonol.

Burroughs realized that he would be Ras Thavas, the Master Mind of Barsoom. Thavas was the likeliest incarnation. He had studied medicine in Vienna. He would have been a doctor if he hadn't spent so much time picking boys in the steam baths. The Red Mist will have carried the drug south to Bradbury City, which would be Helium now. The People's Republic of the South Pole would be filled with Holy Therns and First Born.

The dank air of the Toolonian Marshes began to fill

his mind with memories. Jasoom sparkled brilliantly blue in the west, a newly mysterious world where Opar had supplied gold to lost Atlantis. Perhaps he would visit its interior of Pellucidar or go the second planet and meet the hideous cloud people. He walked toward the family estate, not Cobblestone Gardens built with adding machine money, but Ras Thavas' twenty three thousand year old estate where he would begin to build synthetic men. Here he could study not only humans, but also the four-armed green men and the white apes. Here were the data points he needed, praise Pharol!

Here he would discover the secret of the human vessel.

For PJF, the Jungle Rot Kid, wherever he is.

ABOUT THE AUTHOR

DON WEBB has had sixteen books published, and some of his material has been translated into eleven languages. He fell in love with Science Fiction in grade school, and had his first professional stories published in 1983 in *Interzone*. He is equally attracted to the pre-Golden Era science fiction as he is to the experiments of the New Wave, and tries to synthesize both in his writing. He teaches high school English as well as classes for UCLA extension.

As a Texan, he has a secret chili recipe, enjoys his home in Austin, and has been a fixture for many years at the local SF convention, Armadillocon. He grew up in the days of the 'zine revolution, and has a love for the small press, as well as places that occasionally send him cash. He lives with his lovely wife Guiniviere and two cats. He is not as funny as he thinks he is.

You can reach him at:

writebydonwebb@gmail.com

www.ingramcontent.com/pod-product-compliance
Lightning Source LLC
Chambersburg PA
CBHW020803250626
47155CB00003B/1192

A VELVET OF VAMPYRES

It's a "murder" of crows and a "parliament" of owls. For bats, the genus is "velvet," and hence also for vampires. We like the older spelling, the one John Polidori gave us when he alerted the world to their presence. They're here—dominating our dreams, our fears, our media. But what if they aren't boy-band-pretty with diamond sparkly skin? What if they're more dangerous because they're Desire herself? What if they're behind deep erotic urges AND the desire to write a poem? What if they live in the need to tear open a bright shiny Christams present AND the desire to drink hot red blood burning bright in the night?

Seven great tales of the living undead by a Master of the Order of the Vampyre of the Temple of Set. *Caveat lector!*

Borgo Press Books by DON WEBB

*Do the Weird Crime, Serve the Weird Time: Tales of
the Bizarre*
A Velvet of Vampyres: Tales of Horror
The War with the Belatrin: Science Fiction Stories
Webb's Weird Wild West: Western Tales of Horror

A VELVET OF VAMPYRES

TALES OF HORROR

DON WEBB

THE BORGO PRESS

MMXII

A VELVET OF VAMPYRES

Copyright © 1994, 1995, 1996, 2012 by Don Webb
Cover art Copyright © 2009 by Fergus Fitzpatrick

FIRST EDITION

Published by Wildside Press LLC

www.wildsidebooks.com

DEDICATION

This book is dedicated with respect to
Lilith Aquino.

CONTENTS

ACKNOWLEDGMENTS

"Introduction: Why Vampyres? Why Now?" is published here for the first time. Copyright © 2012 by Don Webb.

"The Most Beautiful Man in the World" was first published in *Dreams of Decadence* (date unknown). Copyright © 2012 by Don Webb.

"Thirteen Lines" was first published in *Blood Muse: Timeless Tales of Vampires in the Arts,* edited by Esther Friesner and Martin H. Greenberg, 1995. Copyright © 1995, 2012 by Don Webb.

"The Lamp" was first published in *The Edge*, May/June 1996. Copyright © 1996, 2012 by Don Webb.

"The Evil Miracle" was first published in *The Magazine of Fantasy & Science Fiction,* August 1994. Copyright © 1994, 2012 by Don Webb.

"Scholomance" is published here for the first time. Copyright © 2012 by Don Webb.

"Kissing Sleeping Beauty" was first published in *Fringeware Review #666*, October 1994. Copyright © 1994, 2012 by Don Webb.

"Poe on the Morning After" is published here for the first time. Copyright © 2012 by Don Webb.

INTRODUCTION
WHY VAMPYRES? WHY NOW?

When John Polidori wrote "The Vampyre" in 1819, he created a lasting genre by remanifesting an old myth. Although centuries of good Christian thinking had done their best to bury the notion we know. We know. We know that the Past wanted to fuck us and suck the life out of us. And although it's scary, we like the notion. As modern humans as we rush about in our daytime world we know that although we are too numbed and scattered to really deeply desire anything, we know that there must have been figures in the past who could have so desired. Odysseus was more clever, Hercules more strong, Solomon wiser. These are acceptable myths. But what of someone or something that craves Life much more strongly than we can? Are they not as likely heroes as well?

Or can deer make heroes of wolves?

Polidori took a few elements of folklore, his own interest in Mesmerism and his unrequited love for Lord Byron and hit the chord. What happens when our unconscious mixes the fear of death, the pang of the loss of loved ones and the desire for the unobtain-

able? It is a powerful and corrosive alchemy—sort of a Jungian Shadow with an Everclear chaser.

The Vampyre rears its lovely head in times of stress. When the objective universe has become overburdened with political, economic and environmental strife, the Vampyre is there. The unspoken longing, "If I could only, just once loose control!" summons them from their crypts and some of our inkbottles.

This small booklet has certain magical properties. If you keep under your pillow after you have read it, you dream of Vampyres. And they will dream of you.

—Don Webb

THE MOST BEAUTIFUL
MAN IN THE WORLD

Her favorite hunting ground was the Café du Monde. She wasn't the only one who preyed there, of course, there are great advantages to tourists as prey. It was an open-air cafeteria for vampires: as they wiped their powdered sugar from their chins and talked about how you couldn't get coffee like this back home, you could size them up. Ever since the place opened in 1862 it had served the needs of the city's undead.

There was a fellow there right now. He had had a hard night, maybe an argument with some friends, maybe a fight with his wife and so he had come down to Decatur Street to stare gloomily into his steaming coffee. He didn't even notice the fat pigeons that landed by the tables, keeping like the café itself a twenty-four-hour schedule.

She would wait till he decided to walk back to his hotel. He didn't look like someone that was staying in the Quarter, probably he had a room in one of the big hotels near the stadium. Sizing up prey was her second favorite part about being a vampire. She fantasized sometime about being a criminal profiler. Mrs.

Sherman was very into criminal profilers. Not a lot of work opportunities for anyone who puts 240 down for age. Unlike some of her kind, she prided herself on keeping some tabs on the human world. It made the stalking better, it made the world more sensible, it made the feeding much, much better.

She was sitting in the shadows in the Square. Nine out of ten people couldn't see her, some people regarded this as a feat of invisibility. She had thought so for years, until she had caught Norbert, that physics students from Tulane. He had known so much! He was the only victim that she had kept alive for a long time. They had had nearly eighteen months together. When she killed him, she had hoped that he would cross over. He was going to write a dissertation on the temporal bio-physics of vampires. Of course, she had to kill him before he had submitted anything to his doctoral committee, such information might be useful to the crowd of want-to-be Van Helsings that hovered around the vampire community like avenging angels. But it had made things so clear when he had told her...

Wait. He's leaving the café now. Let him pass. Walk up from behind.

"Excuse me sir? Are you on the way to the hotel?" she asked.

He turned and took in her auburn hair, her warm brown eyes, her diaphanous dress; and she had seduced him with a glance. It was too easy sometimes.

"Yes, Ma'am. Can I help you?" he said.

"I am worried to be out so late. I had seen you at the

hotel earlier, and I was hoping you could walk me back. I would feel much safer," she said, already putting out her arm for him to take, which he did lightly, and with a smile thinking that he was the hunter not the prey.

"Of course I'll walk you back, Ms—?"

"Burgess," she said, "Sheila Burgess."

They walked and he began small talk. Had she been in the city before? Did she like Bourbon Street? Had she visited the Voodoo Museum? What about the cemetery?

He was boring, so she decided not to spend too long with him. She talked about her knowledge of architecture, about the wrought iron and balconies and the numerous hidden gardens and tiny retreats.

"In fact," she said, "there's a famous courtyard just up that alley. We could look over the fence at it."

They entered the alley.

He said, "I don't see any courtyard, I don't see any fences for that matter."

"Silly I just wanted you off the street for a minute, so I could have you for myself."

She put her arms up as if to draw him close for a kiss, and he bent down. When he passed close enough, she felt her will pouring into his body, holding him still for the feeding. The victim has to give himself willing, but once the gift is made, he is hers.

Her fangs pierced the throbbing artery, and hot life poured into her in great spurts, filling her with what she Needed.

Along with the blood came images, a dream-like

stream of the victim's last thoughts and deeds and dreams. Nothing special here—he was a shoe salesman here for a business meeting, he couldn't sleep, he had a loveless marriage. His image of his wife was so weak that she couldn't see her at all.

The image stream was very unsatisfying, but it was the icing, and she fed for the cake. His blood was healthy, vital and tasty.

He lost consciousness, and fell out of her arms.

She took his wallet. She seldom needed or used cash, but she felt it lessened the chance of him reporting a vampire to the police. He wouldn't remember much, and the missing wallet would answer such questions as he might have or generate.

She stepped back.

There was time for another victim, she had fed, it would have to be someone really special. There was a little all-night café in the garden district. She only went rarely, but she wanted something more exciting than the half-formed dreams of a shoe-salesman chasing around her head as she lay hidden away during the day.

She was about to fly, when she saw him—the most beautiful man in the world.

He had been watching her, standing less than five feet away. He looked full of admiration and maybe a little lust or love or some emotion that she knew from long ago but didn't have a name for now. He had long black hair, and eyes of cobalt blue. He had a slight tan, making him into some sort of pale-dark demigod.

"Hello, beautiful," he said. If anyone anywhere else

had ever said that, she would have laughed, but she felt he meant it, and that she deserved it.

Her first thought was that he was also a vampire. From time to time the undead do seek each other's company, but such relationships are doomed because of the predator's need for resources. Always the hunger gets in the way, always eats love, friendship, art—whatever.

"Hello," she said.

The victim at her feet moaned. She looked down, then back to the beautiful man, but he was walking away.

"Who are you?" she asked.

"I am the shape of your dreams," he said.

She decided not to follow, she had to think. Vampires are a vulnerable lot because of the daily sleep, and the hatred of mankind for their captors.

She decided to call it a night, and flew home.

Home was a tiny boarding house in the garden district. The landlady knew what she was, and thought it was great. The landlady had hopes of being a great horror novelist, and felt the experience of having a vampire tenant would be good on her literary resume.

The landlady was an idiot and Sheila knew she would have to killher someday.

Inside the room with its heavy drapes and dust-covered blinds laythe coffin.

* * * * * * *

From *The Temporal Biophysics of Hemoglobin-*

Consuming Undead by Norbert Neilly (unpublished thesis), p. 14:

The attraction that human beings have toward vampires is not a simple sexual or aesthetic attraction; although such elements may certainly exist. I will show in this paper that the attraction is based on the normal movement of complex systems in time. In short humans are drawn to vampires because the vampire is more closely associated with the field-state called the *future*, than the present. There is a capacity discharge between the human and vampire that allows the human to have the same sort of experiences that they would normally associate with the *future*—that is to say, intense fantasy activity, or, if you will, daydreaming raised a quantum level. The vampire on the other hand has a discharge of the human's past in the form of memories and reveries. This relationship draws the human toward the vampire, by a simple intensification of the force that draws all of us toward the future every day. The vampire is drawn to the human, much as the mind is drawn to past events. This has profound effects on the psychology of both species, often times in ways concealed by themselves. The first study of the micro-tubules which appear to be responsible was by Penrose(1994) and....

* * * * * * *

All day long were half-formed phantoms for shoe salesman life, when dusk came she wanted to wash out

her brain. She would go clubbing and find someone interesting, someone that she could sink her teeth into, as it were.

She choose a skimpy little outfit of green satin that showed all kinds of things when she wanted it to.

She stopped by her landlady's.

"You're going out tonight, aren't you?" her landlady asked with that flair for the obvious that seemed to be her most developed trait.

"Yes, Mrs. Sherman," Sheila said.

"How do you pick out you clothes for hunting?"

Sheila gave a brief description of the idea of looking sexy, when you want to attract men. This seemed novel to Mrs. Sherman, and Sheila wondered for the thousandth time how she had ever managed to find a Mr. Sherman in the first place. Of course Mr. Sherman was long gone by the time Mrs. Sherman had moved to New Orleans from Boston. Sheila often thought that everyone in the city except her was a transplant. Of course she was one of the ver few that still regretted the Louisiana Purchase.

She had taken the name "Sheila Burgess" because she saw it on an envelope she found in Canal Street. Two men, Dick Clark and Ed Something-or-other, had been promising great wealth to Ms. Burgess. She had found Mrs. Sherman a short time afterward. It had been time to move the coffin again. Sheila moved every nine years, it relieved boredom, and perhaps stopped the stake happy. Vampire hunters had never been a problem until about a century ago when Bram Stoker's

novel had come out. That dreadful Rice woman, whom she had met at a party once, had made everything much worse by connecting New Orleans with vampire lore. Since her books the sale of cigarette cases with hidden mirrors had increased disgustingly.

There were great side effects though, there were all these young people called Goths and Emos who wandered around the city *hoping* to be victims, and there were scads of would-be writers *hoping* to somehow tap into the success as though success were a vein. She wondered if she was the only vampire that had a literary landlord, ah well being a muse isn't so bad.

She told Mrs. Sherman that it was time to fly, and the middle-aged matron giggled with delight.

The club was for the Goth crowd. Normally they were pretty dull. The images and dreams that came along with their blood were full of black clothes, black walls, and the disgusting use of black makeup. This monochrome approach to life once again convinced Sheila that she was glad she was dead. However, such clubs did collect a truly delectable food, the young would-be artist, whose blood was seasoned with the holy fire. She loved the blood of poets. One intense young man that she had lost control with and drained last year, had the most searing dreams and images in his blood—so much so that she tracked down his works and read them. She was terribly disappointed, it seemed that his hunger for art was high, but that he regrettably knew nothing of the hard work—the preci-

sion that must match the passion.

She saw a likely fellow almost as soon as she passed in the Black Orchid's portals.

He was even handing a little book to a girl he was trying to impress, who was in turn doing her best unimpressed face.

She walked over.

"Are you the poet?" she said, her eyes big on the chapbook. *Bat Wings and Rose Petals* by Robert Severson. He drew himself up, quite nice looking in his black velveteen suit. "I am the poet," he said. Then the veneer of arrogance broke with a smile, "It's my first book, would you like a copy?"

"Yes," she smiled.

Then they were talking and he was drinking coffee, and she wasn't drinking anything, but that wasn't too odd—half the patrons were trying to give out that they were vampires.

Then she glanced across the room and saw him.

He was in a blue shirt that matched his eyes, and wore a turquoise and silver pendant. He looked fierce and beautiful.

The poet had been speaking, and then noticed her distraction, and started to get up and leave.

"No," she said, "I thought I saw an old friend. I'm new to the city and had been hoping to run into Rebecca." A name picked quickly from the mental hat.

"Oh," the poet kept talking, and she decided to seduce him first, feed and then track down the mystery man.

The poet was soon persuaded to taste the night air, and she soon tasted his rich redness. He was wonderfully full of dreams of pearls given to sweethearts, moonlit nights and white rose petals shaken onto black sheets, and storms in the ocean and Paris in the springtime. She had been to Paris as a little girl. It was different then, she had dreamt of going to see the Eiffel Tower.

He fell gently onto the street. She might drain him all the way to see if he had the strength to pass over. What was it Norbert said about that phase-transition?

He was watching. He had pressed himself against the wall of a building, being at one with its shadows.

When he saw that she saw him, he stepped forward smiling and open.

"Who are you?" she said.

"John Seymour."

"That's very helpful. What are you?"

"A connoisseur of vampirism."

"What if I don't like to be watched?"

"You like to be watched, you dream about it, you fantasize about how good you are, and I must say you are unlike many of the clumsy excuses for vampires I've see, are quite good, and quite beautiful."

"You're very gallant to have such a morbid hobby."

"It isn't a hobby. Here have a picture of me." He reached in his pants pocket and took out a snapshot. It was him standing on Commerce Street in full daylight reading a paper.

She looked up at him to ask another question, but

found herself paralyzed for a moment. When it passed he was gone.

* * * * * * *

The next night, the mystery man was all she could think of. She stood at the street corner in the photo. Sometimes she would fly high above it and watch the streets and alleys. But he didn't come.

The night after that she tried hanging out at the Black Orchid.

The third night she was really hungry, but she made herself feed only in tiny amounts all over the city in the hopes she would find him looking at her.

She wanted him.

Not in the way she wanted a victim; although there was some of that.

She wanted him in the way she used to want a man, if after two hundred years of no human desires her memory was accurate.

It wasn't just sex, it was—well something more.

On the fifth night he found her. She had been heading to the Café Du Monde. He was behind her on Decatur St.

"Ms. Burgess?" he asked.

His voice was warm like the gulf sea she had played in so very long ago.

"Yes," she said.

"Ms. Burgess, I thought about dropping by your home on Chambers St. today, but when I realized that you wouldn't be up."

Fear filled her, she should run, he knew where her coffin was. But his eyes were the eyes of starlight, and she could fear nothing.

"Ms. Burgess, or may I call you Sheila?"

"You may call me Violeta. I was born Violeta Zivie."

"What a beautiful name, the 'veiled one', how fine for someone in whose aspect and her eyes the best of both bright do meet." He said.

"What do you want from me?"

"Everything, really. All the world and time. But I will start with a question: do you miss the day?"

Sheila thought of the warm sun—that great yellow that she had not seen since the early settlement here.

"Of course I miss the day."

"I can give you the day. Well maybe I can give you the day."

"How?"

"I am your future, much as you are the future of men. I feed upon vampires, drawing their rich accumulation of the past. I don't have to feed often, once a decade perhaps. So I spend a long time looking for my prey. I've been watching you for three years, ever since you killed a student of mine at Tulane."

"Norbert. But I—"

"You needn't say anything. He died happy, which is a rare thing in the world of men."

"I had hoped he would pass over."

"I had hoped so too, I would have spent many long nights with him as we would bring science to bear on ancient magics. Oh don't look at me that way, I am

not interested in putting blood in vials and testing my theories on dogs and mice. There is a way to approach magic with science, already half in magic and wholly informed by wonder."

"Did you become what you are through your science?"

"No I was you. I was brought to an even higher realm by a poor mad woman. She never knew what had happened to her, how she reclaimed the day by feeding on her own kind. Trying for self knowledge began my sciences".

"If you drain me, I will be as you?"

"You might. Or you might be a husk that I leave on the street to wait the long centuries looking for one as beautiful as you."

"That doesn't offer me much hope."

"We have never been in the job of offering hope. Only possibility," he said.

"Norbert said that, he said that vampires offer dreams," she said. "What do you get if I die?"

"Nutrition and two hundred years of memories, not just yours, but of all those you have feasted upon."

"And I would get such dreams as you represent."

She thought about it only a moment, and then looking deeply into the cobalt of his eyes, decided they were so deep that the future must live there.

She stepped forward and put her arms around him. She kissed him once, then offered her neck.

"To the future" she whispered.

THIRTEEN LINES

Before I encountered the unfinished sonnet of Henry Salt, I would have said that there was nothing on the world that was worth my life. Everything has changed by my reading the thirteen lines. I now know Love and Terror.

My door into the place of damnation was (appropriately enough) the love of money. I work as a research assistant at the Harry Ransom Center at the University of Texas. We've got quite a collection, including the fine copy of Bram Stoker's *Dracula*; you should stop by some time. My job is to aid those scholars and seekers after the mysteries that visit our air-conditioned halls. Sometimes the work is both hard and exhilarating; sometimes there is nothing to do. Being the thrifty sort that I am, I use my free time to produce little gems of independent scholarship that I sell for small recompense. My real name does not matter, but perhaps you know my pseudonym of John Kincaid, who writes lots of articles of the paranormal or just plain weird.

I had an idea for a honey of an article on strange manuscripts and cursed books. I figured I'd cover four or five texts, plus some pictures and I've got a feature.

Maybe if I played my cards right *Omni* or *Playboy* could be tempted. My formula for success in paranormal writing—what the heck, I can give it to you now that I'm leaving the field—was to cover the same old ground for seventy-five-to-eighty percent of the article, and then add one truly new item. This would make my article hot and quotable and ensure that I could sell my next article.

Very, very few people are aware that I am John Kincaid. It would probably make most researchers uncomfortable. Would you want your research assistant to be the man who wrote "Was Lincoln's Father Bigfoot?"? No, I didn't think so.

My article on mysterious texts covered the magical papyri of Thebes, the Voynich manuscript, and Dr John Dee's "Enochian" cipher. All well researched and well known texts for the occult crowd. I was browsing through the on-line catalog for occult curiosities when I came across *Blood Loss and Poetry: An Account of the Inanna Sonnet* by Austin O. Emme, London, Dawglish & Son, 1925. "An account of the so-called vampire sonnet, its translators since the Middle Ages, and the discovery of the original text in Sumerian, with especial emphasis on the life of Henry Salt, Esq." Private edition of 333 copies. LOST.

The last word dashed my hopes as much as all the others had raised them. LOST meant that the book had been part of one of the rare book collections, and that most likely it had walked away with some visiting scholar. Our current security system prevents any such

thefts, but in a more trusting age—say, thirty years ago—such a stringent system wasn't in place, and the occasional visitor overcome by bibliophilic lust took a book or two. I decided to post queries on a couple of electronic librarian's lists looking for either *Blood Loss and Poetry* or any information on Henry Salt.

Then I went out to lunch.

* * * * * * *

It was a couple of days before I got a response. A couple of postings revealed that Henry Salt had been an undistinguished curator of Egyptian and Mesopotamian antiquities at the Sallust Museum. A third indicated that he had died during a scandal of 1898, and the fourth proved most interesting.

"We too have lost our copy of Austin Emme's book, but one of our grad students in the Sixties had begun a study of "Scarlet Woman Motifs in Ecstatic Poetry" and provides a copy of the vampire sonnet:

'Look into the heart of wind on storm night
'and find a sudden black rainbow.'

Just as I read the first couplet I heard a sudden metallic noise, like a huge wreck, and I ran to my window. Below on Guadalupe Street what had been a small Japanese car and a large four-wheeled Jeep were now one. Three or four other vehicles had hit each other or parked cars in an effort not to smash into the central pair. Students, homeless beggars, street entrepreneurs

were pointing and yelling. Amidst the crowd stood the oldest and ugliest woman I had ever seen. She was dressed head to toe in black, Iranian somehow. Sirens sounded, and I could hear my coworkers going to their windows.

I went back to my terminal, but the screen was blank. Goddamit! Had I hit the delete key or otherwise screwed up? I spent several minutes trying to retrieve the missing message, and wound up sending a note to the computer center asking if they could help me.

I worked till dusk. I had gone through a painful divorce a couple of years ago, one of my best defenses against loneliness is overwork.

It was a beautiful warm Texas night and I didn't want to hurry home. I walked through campus. UT has a beautiful campus, full of Spanish buildings and fountains. I sat on the edge of one of them, where hippocampi sported in the back-lit foam. Very pretty and the white noise filled my ears as spray soaked my tired face....

And I found myself dancing in an old palace all soft stone and candlelight. My partner wore a black veil that shimmered like moonlight on a lake and we danced by vast windows which looked upon a world in perpetual night where the ground outside was white as snow, but I knew it wasn't covered with snow, then my head plopped back and I woke up.

I had fallen asleep by the fountain. I felt dizzy and confused, and very embarrassed. I'm sure I looked drunk or drugged. I stood up, a little bit staggered by

my experience. Someone laughed behind my back.

I didn't feel like driving home, so I decided to return to my office. I was there several minutes before it occurred to me that I might need medical attention. I was frankly hoping to fall asleep again and regain the sweet feeling of the dream.

* * * * * * *

As my orientation returned I decided to check my email. Two more messages on Salt. One was from a colleague in Denver; after pleasantries he got to the point:

"We have the Emme book. Henry Salt went from respected 'Orientalist' (as they said in those days) to a kind of street person. He had acquired a clay tablet bearing a hymn to Inanna, which he translated and then discovered that it matched a medieval French poem. At first he published this as a historical finding—evidence of a poetic tradition going back to the Euphrates. Then he went through a period of trying to form a 'Cult of Insubstantiability' which got him fired from the Sallust. Then he had a change of heart and spent all of his money buying every copy of his articles on the hymn. He even snuck into the Sallust and hammered the tablet to bits. He apparently died in front of the museum a few days later, some said of blood loss. To my surprise I discovered that we've never made a microfilm copy of the book. As soon as we have one made up, I'll send it to you. Thanks for the interesting read."

The other was from the Oriental Institute in Chicago. Its message was more to the point.

"Leave the 'Unfinished Hymn to Inanna' SM 10188 alone. It claims a scholar every couple of decades. Stick with something safe like crack cocaine."

* * * * * * *

Needless to say I was more intrigued than ever. All commercial dreams had vanished. I wanted something that I could know—some Mystery that was for me and me alone. There is nothing that can be possessed as fully as something within one's mind.

I waited daily for the microfilm from Denver, and I continued to have my little dreams. I remembered little of them, save for the slow lovely dance with the veiled woman and the delicious sense of swooning that accompanied each dance. I wanted to have her, take her, but even more than that I wanted to speak with her to know her thoughts and being.

I don't recall ever being so much in love.

Certainly not my marriage to Beth, certainly not in college or high school romances. Never in fiction or movies or fantasy.

My boss called me in and asked what was wrong with me.

How did she mean?

She said that I had been getting really sloppy about finishing assignments. The other day I had been speaking with a man from Utah and that I had just wandered away from him in mid-sentence.

I sort of remembered this, but shrugged it off with a bad joke about Mormons.

She also asked about my health saying that I was looking pale and wan.

I asked if she was worried about expenses for our health plan. It was all in all very unpleasant.

I knew that I could stop, but I wanted to let things goon for a little while at least. I needed a better picture of things, and besides I felt so dreamy.

* * * * * * *

The microfilm arrived. I'll quote from relevant sections.

"Dr. Salt's initial paper on the clay tablet from Persepolis stressed that it was not a fragment—that the poem was actually incomplete. He speculated that this was perhaps the first poem to be written *first*, before being recited—and that the unnamed scribe simply couldn't think of an ending before the clay dried."—p. 14.

"Salt never revealed his sources for discovering the medieval French, ancient Greek, or seventeenth century English versions of the hymn; although the existence of some(but not all) of these translations has been verified. His published remarks merely say that these were brought to his attention in a 'mysterious manner.' This probably marks the beginning of his death as a scholar."—p. 23.

"Little is known of the Church of the Yellow Light. Salt took in members from all races and classes. When

I tracked down members some twenty five years later, most could recall nothing. A few had vague impressions of meeting in a drafty cheap hall that Salt had rented, and watching some sort of magic lantern projections. Fewer still had been so stirred by their experiences to try their hands at Theosophy or various occult practices—but for the most part their whole involvement with the Church had been a particularly obscure dream in their dreary dreamlike existence."—p. 48

"Salt gave many alternative translations for the Hymn to Inanna. Some alternate opening couplets include:

> *She is Thunder, the Perfect Mind*
> *Adversity and Advantage is her Name.*
>
> *Sweeter than my own thoughts is she*
> *She, who invented thinking for me*
>
> *What cost red blood for golden nectar?*
> *What cost the world for splendor?*
>
> *Suddenly a black rainbow in the blue night*
> *and in that other world living gold.*

Clearly these cannot be objective translations from the Sumerian. Salt's own explanation for the variations (he apparently produced 418 of them!) was that the original had been written in 'an unknown tongue'."—p. 52:

"The last meeting of the Church of the Yellow Light occurred on October 16, 1898. Salt had been giving one of his lectures on the insubstantial, when he abruptly seemed to change his views. He began shouting, "No! She's mine! Mine alone!" and chasing people from the hall. The rumor that he later set the hall on fire is unsubstantiated, perhaps this was the work of a disillusioned follower or maybe a random vagrant."—p. 101

"One of the most ingenious theories was that the poem tried to define the undefinable, or as Salt put it, "to make the Unknown Known." Most of the poets or translators had tried to add a word to the poem, some even attempted a whole line. According to Salt, it was the *strain* of extending the poem that caused the blood loss . The Sumerian version was a mere eight lines long. Salt had located an English language version of 1814 consisting of twelve full lines and the beginning of a thirteenth. Salt's final version of the poem was cast in the form of an unfinished sonnet awaiting its fourteenth line. I have published the verse as appendix B to this volume. Although I find the supposed occult or "vampiric" nature of the sonnet to be utter rubbish, I must admit I find the lines lines a bit too fascinating. This no doubt speaks of the suggestibility of the human mind, and perhaps lends support to the theories of Dr. Freud."—p. 135

"Although Salt's death was rumored to he caused by anemia, no autopsy was performed nor medial report of any kind made. The sheriff attributed the death to

exposure. The body was to have been buried in the family vault, but was stolen by person or persons unknown and no doubt performed its last civil service for aspiring medical students."—p. 167

The microfilm broke before I could read the thirteen lines of Henry salt. I had to wait and get help to repair the machine, because I didn't want to risk gumming up the works and possibly loosing my chance to read the microfilm for several days.

While I was waiting for the technician to come to fix the microfilm, my boss sent for me.

She told me that my clothes were dirty. She told me that I *smelled*. She told me that I needed a shave.

She said my eyes looked sunken. Was I *on* something?

She told me to go home.

"But I'm waiting for some film to be fixed."

"It's five o'clock. You can look at it tomorrow—when you come in clean and shaved. Get some sleep. Take a vitamin pill for Christ's sake."

"But this is a very important project. I've been working on it since the day of the big wreck."

"What wreck?"

I began to understand. I went home. I would have to make the decision whether or not to read the poem, because I began to see what the implications were.

* * * * * * *

The woman came to me in a dream that night.

As I had expected.

I found myself in the vast stone hall whose windows looked upon miles and miles of ground as white as snow. I could see the land clearly now; it was covered in bones. The soft glow inside the hall, which I had attributed to candlelight in all my dreamy dreams of love, had no source. It came from everywhere and cast no shadows. As I pondered this, a voice came from behind me—a voice so sweet that I could feel it make my sleeping body shiver.

"The light is the force of Mind. Ultimately it is the only light we have in this darkling universe. It is my light."

I turned to face her. She had removed her veil. I took her in my arms and we began to waltz to silent music. How can I describe her face, a face that has the beauty of a thousand moonlit nights? Or the eyes of a blue not of your earth, for it is such a blue that can only be imagined? Or her hyacinthine black hair, whose luster suggests another spectrum—an anti-light whose unknown colors could only be spread by a prism whose angles are unknown to man?

All of this and so much more was she.

"None of this is real is it?" I asked.

"No. Not in the way you mean real." She said, "This is imagination alone. This is the insubstantial. Yet alter anything here, and those things in that other world which are symbols of here are altered proportionally."

We waltzed and waltzed and stone wall and dark windows spun.

"I am the goddess of this place. I am the source and the Form of all dream lovers. I am real as long as I am loved."

"You are Inanna?"

"I have any name you want to give me."

"And how long would you keep that name? How long would you be faithful?"

"I will be faithful as long as you lived, devoted to you absolutely. My love and lust would be as absolute as could be imagined by anyone, anywhere. For I am the Form of the dream lover."

"And when I died?'

"I would spirit your body here, to lay in the endless lands of insubstantiality. Your bones would join the millions, and I would become the old woman wandering the Earth till another was chosen. One that could see me and my illusions."

"Would you remember me, out of your millions of lovers?"

"No." she said, and I could feel my sleeping twitch with agony, but I did not awaken. She continued, "No, but while we loved the rain of inspiration would fall upon your race. While you struggled to add another line to my poem, a thousand poets would be born. While your blood itself boiled away the idea of Love would become more perfect."

I awoke and I thought of her. I pictured myself crazed and bloodless, trying to live one more day so that I could dream one more night.

I could put it aside. I could throw away the microfilm

and delete my computer files. I hadn't taken a vacation in a couple of years. I could go to Vegas, blow some of that money I'd socked away since my divorce. I could get drunk and go to a cathouse. I could....

I wasn't even fooling myself. Tomorrow I'd shave and bathe, and put on a clean suit. I'd get up early so I could catch breakfast at a restaurant downtown, where I'd have beef steak and eggs Florentine to build up my blood.

And I would read Henry Salt's unfinished sonnet and start to work on the fourteenth line.

THE LAMP

The author dreams of a remarkable object, a hurricane lamp set atop a lead crystal sphere containing auburn hair. The assembly is a bit too tall and dangerous for an oil lamp—it could easily tip over, smash and start a great fire. Upon awakening the author lights the gaslight and begins to write an account of the hairlamp. He intends to weave the hairlamp into his *Mr. Rodger's Neighborhood*, a contemporary novel of Victorian poverty. He sees it as an ending, the lamp can ignite Rodger's house and destroy all loose ends. In his haste he spills ink on his yellow silk pajamas. He finishes his account before the ink dries and carefully removes the pajamas in order to minimize the area of the stain. He reaches for the green velvet pullcord, but decides not to wake the servants. He will carry the pajamas to the laundry.

He dresses. Holding the pajamas over his left arm, he descends the stairs. He sees a light in the entrance hall. He investigates, finding the hairlamp. It matches his description exactly:

"The lead crystal shell is spherical, slightly flattened at its poles. Its diameter is perhaps one foot. Clean

short tawny auburn human hair fills half of its interior. Diamonds have been incised on its surface. Above the shell rests a flat ovoid of deep rose glass which contains the fuel for the lamp. Above the ovoid a tarnished brass collar and above that a quite normal hurricane lamp unusual only in its extreme brightness."

The lamp rested on a dark wooden three-legged table. The author recognized the table as being a piece of dubious stability long ago relegated to the box room. The whole assemblage invited disaster. He thought of calling the servants and demanding the fire hazard be put out of the house; but he refrained feeling somehow responsible for its existence. It probably wouldn't be here when morning comes.

He took the pajamas to the laundry and went very quietly to bed.

* * * * * * *

The lamp remains. He watches the fuel. The lamp consumes almost none. He wonders if he is in the presence of a miraculous lamp like the temple light of the Maccabees. He decides to send for the vicar if the fuel level hasn't dropped an inch by Sunday.

With great cunning and diplomacy he questions the servants. None are aware that the lamp is a new member of the household.

He attends the lamp for a full day. He retires at ten. At eleven his manservant wakes him. His mistress is calling. The author is displeased. Tuesdays have been allotted for sexual congress. He has her sent up.

She rushes into the room and begins disrobing. As a surprise she has shaved her pubis. She has also shaved her head having made a wig of her auburn hair. Now I am completely naked, completely yours, she says. The author is excited and asks her if the hair in the lamp is hers. She gasps she calls him vile and berates him with a string of epithets which he has heard heretofore only from London cabdrivers.

She gathers her clothing and flees the room. He listens until he knows she is out of the house. He rises, puts on his robe, and picks her wig off the floor. He takes it downstairs and compares it to the hair in the crystal shell. The wig is slightly darker. He gives the wig to his manservant. If his mistress should ever call again, give her this.

* * * * * *

Over the next few days his friends stop by on various flimsy excuses. He sees them impatiently unwilling to be apart from the marvelous lamp. He is afraid to move it lest it fall and equally afraid that it will be jostled in the entrance hall. Despite his wishes to the contrary a pressure builds up he must mention the lamp to the visitor. Each guest comments on his vulgar behavior. They are incensed. He cannot understand it. He breaks friendships of years standing one by one until he is utterly alone.

The servants are troubled by vampires. They pale and move slower each day. Finally they creep into the entrance hall and beg for release. The author sitting

on a small chair next to the lamp dismisses them. As an after thought he arranges for one of them to bring his dinner daily from a nearby restaurant, and another to turn off the gas as he won't be needing it anymore. They proclaim that he is the justest, wisest, kindest master they have ever served.

The manservant departs with the wig and marries the mistress, believing it to be his master's wishes.

The author forgets to call the vicar.

* * * * * * *

Several months later another series of visitations begin. Acquaintances from college from school from the Welsh village he grew up in. Each comes in reverse chronological order of his meeting them. The author is able to meet them civilly—fully dressed and away from the lamp. He recognizes the visits are part of the lamp's process. He entertains his guests with great wit apologizing for the lack of servants and the inch-thick dust. Finally they have run their course.

He begins to dream of his auburn-haired mother. Perhaps the hair is hers. After several weeks he gathers his resolve to leave the lamp. He travels to his uncle's home where his crippled father lives.

His father tells him that his mother was blonde not auburn. His father begs him for a room in his London home. The author agrees but asks a month to put things right.

He returns to London. He grabs the lamp and hurls it into the street. He sighs a great sigh as every muscle

and nerve relaxes for the first time in nearly a year. The great sigh puts out the fire in the street. He goes upstairs to sleep.

He dreams of a yet more remarkable object.

THE EVIL MIRACLE

Martha Wills made the down payment on the Starlight Motel in 1966 in memory of her only love. Now in 1992 she is sixty-seven and wondering if there is a chance of selling it in a terrible real estate market. And there are the spiders.

The tarantulas—big furry black ones—had always been a problem. Just one of them padding across the asphalt would bring a Yankee tourist screaming for his (or more likely his family's) life. Across the highway the old prairie dog town was full of 'em, and they became quite frisky in the warm weather. Martha knew them as harmless. You damn near had to step on one to get him to bite you. As a child she and her brother Billy used to fish 'em out of holes with bubble gum. You'd get your well-chewed bubblegum—long, dangly, and pink—and you'd lower the string into a prairie dog hole. You'd pull up a tarantula and swing 'em around— sort of a living hairy yo-yo. Tourists didn't relate well to this story. Next were the garden spiders. Black and white wonders of the spider world, they could've been designed by Picasso. They spun huge webs to glisten rose window-like with the morning dew. Usually she'd

have one on the roses out front and one in the bear grass out back. But this year they were everywhere—linking guests' cars with their sticky floss; obscuring doorways; filling the aluminum steps which led to the diving board of her pool. Martha had taken to getting up at dawn and dewebbing the place.

Finally there were the brown recluses. A different matter. They were one of the truly poisonous species. The bite could be fatal. Martha's cousin was once bitten. The tissues of his leg turned black and smelled of rot. When—months later—Robert had healed, he was missing a handful of leg. The tiny brown recluse likes to sleep in shoes and other tight places. Martha had found six in the twenty-seven years she owned the Starlight. Three of the six she had found last month. She figured that the spider increase was somehow due to pesticide use. She'd half-slept through a made-for-TV movie with that theme. She didn't tell anyone about the spiders. She didn't want rumors to start. Brown recluses could kill. In the days when the Starlight catered to an interstate tourist trade, a death would have meant nothing. Somebody from New York/Ontario/Alabama died. So what? Who cares? But the small patronage the Starlight now enjoyed was connected to the hospital. Her clients were the families of the patients. They came in from nearby little towns and left after cures, deaths, or loss of hope. But they recommended the Starlight to their plagued neighbors. Cheap and clean, they said, in walking distance of the hospital and the McDonald's. One death from spiders—or even the notion that such

a death was likely—would close the Starlight by the same word of mouth that kept it open.

Martha hadn't told her niece or her nephews that she was going to sell the Starlight. If she told them—she'd have to do it. 'Cause she's that way. Women don't make it in the business world if they appear indecisive. It was like Mr. Rheims said, you have to have fire in your heart and ice in your veins. Mr. Rheims represented the appearance of love to her. Perhaps she even loved him. His name was John.

It was early in the morning and the maids hadn't arrived. Martha turned on the lawn sprinklers. Just so. Any more and people's cars would get wet, any less and the grass wouldn't. She said good morning to Mrs. Abrams, who was already on her way to sit in the ICU waiting room. Promised her that she'd pray for Mr. Abrams. She removed the web across the office door and went inside to make her first pot of decaf.

Across the quiet highway she noticed one of her guests doing something very strange.

The fellow had checked in over a week ago. Martha had been preparing for bed—the Starlight hadn't had a night clerk in three years—when someone hit the buzzer in front. Wearing her peach-colored fuzzy bathrobe, she had checked him in. He wore this khaki outfit; if he had had a pith helmet, she would've sworn he was on safari. He had known her name.

"You're Martha Wills, right? That's what I was I was told, Martha Wills."

It was late and she hadn't asked who or why, but she

wondered. Folks always talk about the Starlight, never about Martha. She didn't think anyone had mentioned her by name since she won $100 by being the ten thousandth customer at a Food King.

But the strange man in khaki—what was his name?—was picking up bits of spider web with tweezers. He was putting the webs in some kind of tiny glass test tube. One strand per tube. He capped each tube with a black rubber stopper, then carefully put the tubes into a case specially fitted to hold them.

Her secret was out. This was some kind of scientist here to study the spiders. Her heart sped up. Her doctor had told her to avoid excitement and coffee. Her heart sped up and this scared her. It was almost a pain to feel this feeling in her chest.

She gripped the smooth wooden counter with the thumb and index finger of her left hand. She could feel her pulse through her fingertip. She would have to relax—have to use the method she learned at Amarillo Community College. Relax, now, relax. Relax between each beat. When she felt calm, she looked at the tar-brown nail of her thumb and wished for the millionth time she could give up smoking.

She couldn't see the strange man from the window of the motel office.

His name was Olin Fletcher, and immediately it became Dr. Fletcher in her mind.

. She decided to call a realtor that afternoon. The realtor came along with a photographer. He shot the Starlight from several angles while his boss drank

iced tea with Martha. They agreed on the truths and lies that could be used to sell the motel. The realtor cautioned her against any kind of For Sale sign. That almost always scared away guests. In fact, Martha might want to run some undetectable promotion to fill up the units. The realtor couldn't promise a sale—it was a slow market—but if Martha could wait six to twelve months, the realtor was willing to work with her. Then the realtor mentioned a figure. It was twenty thousand more than Martha was even hoping for. She should've come to this decision long ago. The realtor also told Martha that the housing market was worse, and when the time came to move from the Starlight she was sure she could find Martha an affordable house in town.

Move from the Starlight. She hadn't quite figured that part yet. Damn Dr. Fletcher.

She served the realtor some carrot cake. She bought it from a shop in town and carefully put it on her grandmother's green platter. Everyone thought it was her own. She pushed her gold-rimmed spectacles up the slope of her sweat-shiny nose. She looked outside and saw that Dr. Fletcher was pestering the photographer. Fletcher had finally donned a pith helmet. What did he think he was—on safari? Trying to talk the photographer into shooting some footage of the quaint aboriginal motel? Please, God, don't let him say anything.

She'd lost track of what the realtor was saying; and now the realtor was leaving, and she hoped she didn't look like a senile fool. Dammit she wasn't old. She

was just distracted. She'd always been distracted by the Starlight.

The realtor and the photographer left. Martha heard the doors slamming shut on their white station wagon—the sound of the gravel as they sped off in the dry Texas heat. She wondered if she had agreed to anything. This was the worst it had ever been. She was letting words make solid life decisions for her and she didn't even know what the words were. She'd let her life drift into this state of disconnectedness. She was worse off than the Starlight. Both were real only in the past, sharing the fate of ruins-- sagging shapes and spiders.

She would put a few things to right, though, and one of them would be Dr. Fletcher.

* * * * * * *

Her chance came two days later. Fletcher stood in front of the Starlight on the tiny strip of Bermuda grass that separated the asphalt of the parking lot from the asphalt of the highway. He admired the burnt orange sunset broken by the Spanish tile roof of the Veterans Hospital. He must have heard her walk up behind him for at the perfect moment he waved his right arm to the sky and said, "It looks like an opened paradise."

She almost fell backwards, because the same words had been said to her twenty-seven years before. Her blood must've collected in her feet, which suddenly seemed made of lead, and her voice must've gone there too for when she spoke she had to lift each word against

the gravity of the whole earth. "How poetic," she said, and thought it was the most stupid and flat thing she have ever said in her life—save for when she had said those same words twenty-seven years before. And then it had been worse because she had said them to a man whom she had just fallen in love with. A Miata whizzed by with its bass so loud she could feel it in her hollow chest. She looked hard at this strange man in the safari suit. It couldn't be the same man. He had his height, but it couldn't be the same man. It couldn't be the same man, because this man brought fear and disappointment and the other had brought love and hope. It was a terrible thing to be an innkeeper because your guests were always bringing you emotions from their strange, far-off lands.

"You think so?" he said, "I'm a lonely man and lonely men are given to poetry."

She would break the pattern. She would say something different. She had to remember. Ah! she knew—comment on something new.

"I like the way the orange light shines on the metal of the new water tower," she said. It was awkward as hell, but at least it was original.

He looked at her with his little green eyes filled with hate. She knew she had stopped him at some game he was playing, but she wasn't sure that she had done a good thing.

"The man taking pictures told me that you were going to sell this place."

"Are you interested in buying it?" I wouldn't sell it

to you for a ka-zillion dollars, she thought.

"Me. No. Even as interesting a site as it is," he shook his head, "It would tie me down too much."

He turned to face the Starlight, and she automatically turned as well. Together they began walking toward the office.

"Could I get you something? A Coke? I like to do special things for my customers who stay for weeks." She would find out his game.

"Not yet," he said. "Not yet."

And before she could say anything else, she saw Mrs. Abrams walking like a wooden zombie. Her cheeks were shiny with tears. Martha remembered that she hadn't prayed for Mr. Abrams. She went toward the grieving woman immersed in her real life's work. It was only much later after she had literally tucked Mrs. Abrams into bed that she thought of the meaning of "Not yet, not yet."

* * * * * * *

Martha's relatives came the next day and it was like a funeral.

She had called them at eleven o'clock in the morning—her nephews Bill, at his dry cleaning shop, and Ralph, at the Frame-It-Yourself in the mall; and her niece Sarah, at the Credit Bureau. Apparently the three of them had decided among themselves that if Aunt Martha ever sold the Starlight, she must be in bad health and soon to die. Or at least soon to be a burden. Sarah, along with the two nephews, drove up in her

slate-blue Ford Escort. They stayed inside the car for a few minutes talking among themselves. Martha watched them through the office's bay window.

When they came in they talked too loud as though she was deaf. They were overly solicitous. They kept telling her to sit down and not to fuss. Sarah's mouth said that Aunt Martha could come live with her; although Sarah's eyes said she would rather go to the dentist seven thousand times instead. Bill and Ralph were full of information on the wonderful retirement communities the city had to offer. It seems that there is the place that began as a sort of apartment—"Just like being a guest at the Starlight"—and then as she deteriorated she could be eased into nursing home-type care. A simple gentle process perfectly tied with the dimming of the light.

She told them that she was getting her own house. A house away from them. They could just leave. And she cried and they left.

This had never happened before.

She had just called them out of courtesy; they had no place in her life. If John hadn't left. No.

* * * * * * *

She had been with him a month in 1966. He had brought her love and mystery and magic. She'd been a maid then and the Starlight a more prosperous establishment living on the lifeblood of Route 66. He had changed her life so much that she knew she would have to hold onto this place.

He had told her that a certain kind of man meets a certain kind of woman and both are changed by the experience. This can happen at the most unlikely places, but at likely times. There is a time when a man has reached a certain stage of his personal development—that only a certain woman could excite love, imagination, and will.

And for that woman, of course, there was only that certain man.

After they had known each other for a week (and had only made love once), he took her to a used book store and bought her a copy of Goethe's *Faust*. He read to her about Gretchen—not at the beginning of the play, but at the end. When Faust's damnation is near—when he had pushed his powers and knowledge to the max and only Hell awaits. Yet Gretchen's prayers open Heaven's gate for him. Her love and constant devotion translate him to a state of glory and knowledge of God.

But Faust abandoned Gretchen, she had said.

"He did what he had to do," he said. "He stuck to his quest."

"But he was evil," she said.

"He sought knowledge and power. Is that evil? Perhaps it's just breaking the human horizons. Galileo was evil when he moved the center of the universe from the earth to the sun. From that understanding we have the space program. Someday we'll even have a man on the moon. Is it evil to want knowledge and power? We send our kids to college so they can get an education and a good job. Our nation is full of tiny Fausts, but we

have forgotten the importance of love in the equation."

He had said many strange and wonderful things and she knew how Eve felt listening to the Serpent in the Garden. Early on she realized that he would someday abandon her. She didn't think it would matter. Although she had never known love before—she had known sex and she had known friendship—she thought that knowing how to love is enough. She would take that knowing and use it on an appropriate man. None of these mystery men stopping in for love and magic. She had tried. After that morning when she woke up alone, and realized that it was really so—she tried. She tried finding other men—men whose place was inside the city. She tried with men she met through singles bars, churches, adult educational programs. There were wild times, fast times, hard times but no love.

She tried to forget about John Rheims. But everything that called to love, the love songs on the radio; a dingy Valentine card found in the street; the sun in the sky; put John's face in her mind.

Had it really been love? Could there have been love in such a short time? And if he really felt the way she did, could he have left her? These questions were with her always.

Three months after John's departure, she won a magazine distributor's sweepstakes. She bought the Starlight from her boss, who was able to fulfill his lifelong dream of retiring to the Hamptons. While he contemplated the cold North Atlantic, she read detective novels and tried their methods at the scene

of the crime.

For the first three years she was too busy to do anything except hope for his imminent return. The address in the register proved to be false, but she hoped that he would prove true. For the next three years she took to asking traveling salesmen and other professional vagabonds if they'd ever met anyone like John. Then she bought the property next door—put in sixteen more units and a restaurant, and for six years she made money hand over fist. She worked all the time and didn't think much. She invested her money wisely. When her brother drank himself to death, she was able to send her nephews and niece to college. Good colleges, too. A few months before her establishment was totally by-passed by the new business loop, she sold the restaurant and the sixteen units to her competitor next door.

The kids came back from college and six quiet years passed. She developed herself. She learned to paint. She took night classes at the community college. She hired herself three assistant managers and she permitted herself a couple of vacations. She woke up one morning and was surprised to see her mother in the mirror—so she stopped looking for love. It just wasn't dignified somehow. These were the years of the secret. She told no one of John, and if anyone remembered the name she advised them she was well over that. She thought that if she spoke not—the memory would lessen. Yet by hiding the secret in silence—it grew ever stronger until it became the driver of her life.

During the eight years that followed, as the Starlight began its decline, Martha pulled her money out. She never let the place get run down or shabby—after all she lived there and one should take care of one's own environment. But she let some of the staff go, she put more of her own salary into T-bills, she created the economic means to live out her life.

She had been thirty-nine when she met John. Now she was sixty-six. She was still surprised when she qualified for a senior discount. Someone would die in a dramatic fashion, and on the news they would say, "an elderly woman." And Martha would find out that the woman was her age. Several friends from her high school class had shown up in the obituaries.

She should have had the answers by now. Instead, terrifying events were threatening the order she took for granted.

* * * * * * *

She didn't sleep.

Her arthritis was bad.

She felt somewhat better after a long hot shower. She wanted to confront Dr. Fletcher at dawn—or as soon thereafter as she could.

She knocked on his door at 6:50. She knew she was waking up other guests, but she plain didn't care. She knocked, waited, knocked, waited, and put her pass key in the lock. Just as she turned the key a chittering noise came from within. Her nerve failed. Dr. Fletcher said, "Later, Ms. Wills, later." She went back to her

room and threw up.

There was someone in the office wanting to check out—pissed off by the early morning knocking. Martha Wills' reflection was pale and sweaty in the office window.

The day was long and she didn't eat anything. At sunset she ventured outside. He was standing on the strip of grass between the parking lot and the old highway again. She was weak and keep falling in and out of visions from her past. Whatever unknown lodestone drew her to this meeting, it had overcome her will. Fletcher raised his arm to the magnificent sunset, "It looks like an opened paradise."

"How poetic," she said.

"I'm a lonely man and lonely men are given to poetry," he said.

"It seems that poetry should attract the perfect audience."

Fletcher turned to her and said, "Now, Martha Wills, now. We have said the words and you know and believe that these words are not said here and now by accident."

"I know and believe," she said, and suddenly everything had that slow-moving clarity of a dream.

They walked back to his room. She sat on the green vinyl chair and he took a small brass jar from his suitcase on the dresser. The jar was simple and unadorned. It looked like an old-fashioned jelly jar save for its material. It seemed very old. He unscrewed the jar, it made a noise like a scratchy 78 on her grandmother's

Victrola. The noise was John Rheims' voice. He said, "You know, Martha, I only want one thing."

"I know," she said.

"The jar," said Dr. Fletcher, "always makes those sounds. I found it ten years ago in a market in Marrakesh. I've spent ten years trying to find out what it means. I can't tell you the number of nights I've spent turning the lid again and again. To find why the jar said these things, I studied phonics, statistics—at first it was a hobby. Then an obsession. Eventually I had to learn the hidden lore of mankind, and I can tell you that it is a good thing that many things are hidden."

"So you found out about John and me," she said. "Let me ask you something. Do you love your little jar?"

"It tortures, it tantalizes. For awhile I thought I loved it, but what it woke up in me is curiosity. All of the strange and beautiful things in my life came from my quest. Even now I don't know what's in the jar. It won't open. The recording principle is simple—the technology is mysterious because of reasons of metallurgy. I've had offers of thousands of dollars from material scientists for my jar. So do you know what the words mean?"

"I know," she said. "But you haven't told me about the spiders."

"They always show up," he said. "They're always waiting when I get to a place. I don't know how the spiders fit in. They're another piece of the puzzle; so what do the words mean?"

For the first time she saw another human being in

Fletcher. His green eyes were alive with want. This was someone who was like herself.

"I know," she said. "But you must tell me where John is. I think I even understand the spiders."

"I don't know. A magician of Marrakesh, who lived in an artificial cave beneath the city, recognized the voice. He said that it belonged to someone who stood outside the circles of time—a voice sometimes heard in the wind at the sacred sites of the most ancient cities. What does he want?"

"He wants my forgiveness."

"Will you give it to him?"

"He is a devil, an evil man. He revolted against God, having to know everything. But I learned love from him and not from God."

"I learned curiosity from him. I had to track down hundreds of people to reconstruct your first meeting."

"Play the message again," she said.

He spun the lid on the small brass jar, "You know, Martha, I only want one thing."

"And the lid never comes off?"

"Just round and round. I'd thought of removing it by force, but I might destroy the very mystery I'm seeking to answer."

Martha pulled herself up in her chair. She sat in a very dignified manner with her hands on her lap. "Play the message again."

"You know, Martha, I only want one thing."

"I forgive you for leaving me John and I hope you have found what you sought."

There was a slight metallic ping! from the jar. Fletcher started to twist at the lid, but stopped himself. He had been so long apart from h is mystery, his beloved, that he had to force himself to stay separate. He managed to ask, "You said you knew about the spiders."

"I had forgotten. I don't know how I had forgotten this with months of spiders showing up to change my life. John has reached out to change my life again. I guess I'm ready for retirement. I guess I'd been waiting to say the words, too. He used spiders as a metaphor for his Work. He said that spiders were perfect Faustian creatures. They make their own worlds out of the material in their blackhearts. Each is its own god; I objected to the metaphor. I told him that God had foreordained each spider to weave its web. Those perfect patterns of symmetry that catch the morning sun are examples of God's will. He said, 'I'll show you some real magic sometime. I'll get spiders to make something other than a preordained web.'"

Fletcher gave the lid another turn. It came off. The jar was empty, but the room was suddenly filled with the fragrance of roses.

Then from beneath the bed, from behind the curtains, from underneath the crack of the door—they came. Spiders. Thousands, maybe millions of them. Fletcher dropped the jar and they scurried over to it. The jar was soon covered.

The swarming mass was organizing. Tarantulas at the bottom, garden spiders in the middle, brown recluses at the top. The mass split into three almost

perfect balls one atop the other.

Fletcher looked at Martha and Martha looked at Fletcher.

There weren't any more spiders coming in.

Martha rose. The spider snowman stood a foot taller than her. She walked to it, and after a moment of dreadful deliberation—stuck her left hand into the center of the garden spider ball. It felt lacy and dry inside—like sticking her hand into a pile of feathers. She felt around—seeking the jar, which she presumed to be in the center. Her fingers found something long and smooth. At first she thought it was a pencil. As she grabbed it her index finger was pricked by something sharp—or maybe a spider had bitten her. She pulled it out carefully.

In her left hand she held a single perfect black rose.

SCHOLOMANCE

The first surprise was that they didn't meet in a castle. It was a simple stone building rather like a monastery, with simple rooms, tiny rooms, to sleep in, and a large common area where they ate and discussed the Secrets of the universe.

When Robert first arrived, he couldn't believe he had found it. Twenty men and women sat around a couple of long tables speaking English. He had expected the classes would be in Romanian or Latin, and had spent years learning both. The door was open.

He walked in with his backpack.

"Is this—?" suddenly he felt really silly. This couldn't be it.

"Is this what, young man?" asked a handsome dark-haired man about his age.

"Is this Scholomance?" asked Robert.

"The Black School? The Devil's Academy? Why yes, it is," said the man and everyone laughed.

"Welcome you're the tenth," said a blonde woman with a trace of a French accent. Everyone laughed again. Robert quickly recounted the number of people in the room—they were twenty-one counting him.

"That's it. 'Welcome'?"

A pale thin woman with butch hair said, "That's it. Now sit. Some of us don't have time to waste."

"Ah," said the silver-haired man at her side, "That brings up a very good point, the need for urgency in the life of a magician."

There followed a long discussion about time, objective and subjective. The discussion ranged over modern physics such as Jack Sarfatti's theories of backwards causality to pre-Avestan Iranian concepts of time. It was fascinating, hard to follow, and not exactly what Robert was expecting from the Devil's School.

After the discussion on time, a red-haired man with glasses that Robert thought looked like a Norwegian schoolteacher said very loudly, "We need a book on time." Then he struck the table with his bare fist thirteen times. No one acted as though this was odd behavior.

At dusk they prepared dinner. Robert saw that only ten of the students ate.

About an hour after dusk the woman with the butch hair approached him. "It's time for bed, I'll show you what you need to do."

She took him down the corridor.

"Your room is here. When you get in, bar the door. Someone will knock at the morning," she said.

"You've got to tell me what's going on here," he said.

"You know what's going on here. This is the Black School, Scholomance. You knew that at the door. You had to track us down. That's the tuition—only people

with enough magical curiosity can find us. There were no walls keeping you out. You're here because of *Dracula*. You read the book, probably as a teenager, am I right?"

"Yes, and—" he began.

"You don't need to tell me," she said, "because we all have the same story. You wanted to live forever. You read that Dracula didn't become a vampire because someone bit him. He learned the arts of magic and alchemy at the Scholomance. Most people figured that was some weird legend that Stoker stuck in the book. But you were different. You looked into Dracula and his story, and the Order of the Dragon and a few other stories that were dark and mysterious, and you figured out that there must have been a Scholomance, a place where cosmic secrets were whispered, where the art of making dreams come true existed. So you came. You had to spend every single cent you owned, didn't you?"

"Everything. When I arrived in Rumania I had one hundred dollars left."

"Now you'll learn the Secrets, maybe you'll pay the price."

"The price?"

"You weren't very good at your research were you? That's probably why you were the last. The class graduates by tens. When the old class is ready to leave, the tenth member of the new class shows up. The old class walks out the door—except for one which a dragon claims. The dragon and student fly straight to hell, where the devil continues their education. He or she

becomes the devil's aide-de-camp."

"But there are twenty-one people here."

"One of them is the devil's agent on Earth. The old ten know who, we don't. Now it's time for bed. Bar your door."

"What if I don't?"

"When a Rule is broken, everyone knows who broke it. Those aren't pleasant days."

He went inside and he barred his door. The room was small, damp, dank, and cold. He began to question himself again on the wisdom of what he was doing. These people seemed intelligent, but they clearly weren't the masters of the universe. And the stuff about a dragon, that had to be symbolic of something. Dracula meant "dragon." He was probably supposed to figure out the allegory. It was a test.

Robert really did want to know the secrets of the universe. He had given up a promising career in physics to be here. He had given up his girlfriend, his family, everything—and journeyed to an obscure village in the middle of Romania to sleep in a tiny cold cell.

He was hurt when the woman said his research wasn't very good. He had found his way here, damn it, he was the tenth. He would puzzle it all out.

He didn't even notice falling asleep.

He found himself in the hall with the others. Great red torches filled the room with a bloody light. There was music and there was a dance around a central cauldron. In the cauldron was fire and black water, mixing and steaming. They're making flame stew, he thought.

The blonde woman came up to him, and kissed him. At first lightly, then deeply. "You're mine," she said, "you're my ticket into the great beyond."

Suddenly he was filled with the most intense lust he had ever felt. He wanted her. Wanted her here. On the floor in front of everyone. Right now.

But the scene shifted and the two of them were flying through the blackness. A wild wind on their bodies, itself as lustful as they, touching them like hundreds of fingers, carrying them. The lascivious wind carried them with great speed toward a darker darkness. A darkness that was so far beyond black that it was luminous with an anti-light.

A great winged beast, with a long sinuous tail, and a great fanged mouth. It must have been a mile long.

"This is what we fear," she whispered to him. "It will take the best of us. It is the shape of one that joins us in our talks. It is all Desire."

The great dragon was beating its wings creating a vast rush of air.

"It flies constantly. It is too full of want to ever settle. Touch it. It's not at its feeding time, now. It's safe."

They flew closer to the dragon and Robert put out his hand to be brushed by the leathery wing.

God it burned, it burned. It burned with every time Robert had wanted to get laid, it burned with every time he wanted learn something, it burned with every juicy fear he had ever had listening to a ghost story, it burned with his desire to tear open bright shiny Christmas presents, to set off fire crackers, to go to the

Moon. It burned and hurt, and felt better than anything he had ever felt. It told his soul that there were other ways to be. That there was a trans-human condition that could let you indulge in all of these desires at once—a multi-dimensional state that accomplished all the powers of the Flesh at the same time. It was eternal and insatiable. It was the fire of Hell and the glory of desire.

Above all things Robert knew he wanted this. He knew he had to some extent because that had empowered to make the long hard journey here, and that little bit of the flame had opened him for more of it.

He turned toward the woman and he felt himself sprouting wings. He saw that she was as well, and then with a spasm of lust that would have rocked a continent she smiled and he saw the fangs.

What they did next could be described as making love, much as Niagara Falls could be described as "fast moving water."

After scores of climaxes they fell to earth. They were human in shape now and they began walking toward the school. Robert noticed that other pairs were approaching the school as well.

She walked with him to his room.

"Tomorrow," she said, "you won't be able to speak of any of this."

Then she pushed him roughly toward his door, and he went right through it and woke up.

The rest of the night he was awake wondering if it had been a dream.

In the morning a knock came on the door and he joined the others for breakfast.

He started to ask about his dream, and found he couldn't open his mouth. He looked over at Ingrid, who merely smiled at him. The only "hard" evidence was that his left hand still hurt where he had touched the dragon.

After breakfast he learned their names. The blonde woman was named Ingeborg, the brunette with the butch hair was called Anne. Swen was the red-haired man he labeled the Norwegian school teacher, the silver-haired gent with the meerschaum pipe was Raoul, and the man who looked to be his own age was Abraham.

They cleared the dishes and Swen picked up a big book that was on the table.

"When we need a book, we ask. It comes to us in the night," he explained.

The text was in Latin, Robert and Raoul translated parts of it.

It described Time as something not natural. There was natural time, of course, the seasons—the movement of the earth. But the time as experienced by man was not natural. Time went by too slow or too fast for man. It was up to man to learn to bend time to his will. Time was described as a great dragon whose mighty wings created time by flapping.

Robert thought that surely as he read that aloud to the group someone would betray themselves. He looked up, no one seemed near to say anything, even Ingeborg.

They had a light lunch and Robert decided he would try steering the discussion. He chose the topic of why the Black School was here rather than say in Paris or New York.

There were many opinions. It had to be some place that was hard to find, that filtered out candidates. It was here because of Bram Stoker's book, if it moved someone would need to write a new book. It was here because of Bogomil heresy, which was connected with the Order of the Dragon to which Vlad Tepes belonged. All of the arguments were sound, so Robert tried his luck. He struck the table thirteen times with his fist and said, "We need a book on the location of the Black School."

He felt silly for doing it. Nothing seemed to have changed, other than his hand was now sore from striking the table. He had expected some cosmic feeling, some notion that what he had done had sent infernal creatures flying off to strange hidden libraries.

However no one looked askance at him, so he figured he had done right.

When bedtime came, he didn't bar his door. He waited till a couple of hours had passed and then opened his door and went to the common hall.

It was dark, no red torches.

He was about to leave when the wind began to blow. It wasn't coming from the open door. It seemed to be blowing *through* the walls. It was a loud wind, full of voices. He thought he heard Ingeborg. She was yelling that he was an idiot. He could hear laughter. The wind

was all around him, but unlike the night before did not pick him up. Then as quickly as the wind had come it was gone.

He remained in the hall. The book from the day before was still there. He lit a candle and read from it. He wanted to be around when the mysterious librarian made the delivery.

The book said the way to beat the dragon of time was to become a creature like the dragon of time. If one (through a process of will and certain arcane formulas) became like the dragon, a maker of time, a certain immortality could be attained. A creature of pure desire, of pure lust for life could not die. Death could not find its way into such a being's burning skin.

Robert was nearing the sections on the formulas when the candle blew out.

The wind was back, full of ecstatic cries and pleasant moans. It blew down the corridors, and was gone.

It was four thirty in the morning. He decided he would slip back to his room and bar the door. No one would be any wiser.

He rose with the rest of them. There wasn't much talk at breakfast. No one would look at him. No one would answer any of his questions. When Ingeborg came in she slapped him. Full and hard.

When it was time for the discussion, he saw that no new book had been brought in the night.

"We'll be discussing your topic tomorrow, I hope," said Abraham. "Please leave us for the day."

Robert thought about protesting, but the cold hate in

their faces told him it wouldn't do any good.

He left the school and spent the day in the village. His Rumanian lessons paid off. He got to meet people at the local bar. He hinted that he was looking for a school.

The region was too poor for a school that foreigners would be interested in.

He hinted that he might be looking for a ruined monastery.

The villagers knew of no such thing.

In fact they seemed blissfully unaware of the Black School. It was the opposite of the movies, where when you mention the name "Dracula" and all the natives cross themselves. After a while he did mention Dracula. Oh, they said, that was in another part of Romania. It was great for the tourists. They needed something like that here.

"What about the building on the outskirts of town?"

They didn't understand him. They liked him as long he was buying rounds of drinks, but they didn't know of any such building. Was it perhaps a language problem?

Slowly it dawned on Robert that they actually didn't see the building. Maybe it was not quite on this earth.

The villagers came to the conclusion that Robert was the advance agent for a Hollywood screen company wanting to film another version of *Dracula* or at least some vampire flick. They began telling him how beautiful their barns were, or how atmospheric their Church. They began following out of the bar, so Robert tried an

experiment. He wanted to see if they could follow him to the Black School.

Sure enough, as they got closer they began giving excuses. One mother had to go home to feed her child. A man would see him tomorrow, he had to go to dinner. One by one they left him. He tried to get the last man to follow him promising money for a vague favor, but as they drew uptown the school the man felt ill. His stomach ached, he could go no further.

Something kept them out, just as something welcomed Robert.

They were at dinner and they motioned Robert to sit. They were cold, but not as cold as during the day.

Robert learned some things about the school.

English was used because it was the most commonly held language. Everyone guessed that it had been French in the last century, and Latin for many centuries before that.

Just before they retired, Raoul asked him very pointedly if he had learned his lesson.

"Yes. I won't make things bad for the others."

That night he dreamed again. He found himself wandering thorough a great graveyard incomparably ancient. As he walked through the stones and cracked mausoleums he could hear weeping, but he could see no one.

Then there she was surrounded by a circle of white candles, her gold hair like a flame. Ingeborg.

"I am so glad that you are not an idiot tonight. It is our last night, so I wanted to be together."

"What did you mean when you said 'I was your ticket'?"

"I was the tenth. One can not pass beyond before one has passed on the essence of the vampire. I gave you the essence. It burns in your veins now. See."

She touched him, ever so lightly opening his wrist. His blood felt like it was boiling, but it was a fire of orgasm, not of earthly kindling.

"The essence is what will transform you. The talks and the texts are supplemental."

Robert leaned forward to kiss her.

It was a long time before either of them spoke.

"What is this place?" Robert asked.

"It is the graves of our loved ones. When you take up the path of personal immortality, you will see countless people you love age and die," she said.

Robert could hear the sound of wings overhead. Great giant wings.

She looked up, "We can't see him here, but he is getting ready to choose one of us as the devil's aide,"

"Will I see you after you graduate?"

"If I am not chosen and you are not chosen, then we can spend all of time together."

"I want that. I want that more than the things I wanted when I came here."

"I want it too, more than anything."

He held her warm soft body as hard as he could, and the vision passed and he found himself back in his cell.

The next day he again found he could not speak of the events of the night.

A book had shown up, this time it wasn't an ancient mysterious tome, it was a simple trade paperback, *The Hidden Tradition in Europe*.

He picked it up.

"I don't believe this," he said. "A paperback?"

"You are very foolish," said Milto. "Truth is where you find it. Most of the great secrets that can be talked about are hidden in books now. You respect the ancient book, but not the modern scholar. You are very foolish."

Robert handed the book around and read how an Iranian time heresy called Zurvanism wound up in Rumania, where it was connected to the cult of the dragon, locally know as the Ismeju. When the name was mentioned several shuddered, Ingeborg among them.

After lunch, Abraham began addressing them, "Tonight ten will walk out that door. One of them will be chosen by the Prince of Darkness. The others will in a real sense never leave this place. Look over the door. *Entres tua anima peretur*. You read Latin, don't you, Robert?"

"'You come in and your soul is lost.'"

The new ten talked to the old ten, thanking them for their guidance. Robert just held hands with Ingeborg saying nothing.

As darkness fell no candles were lit, no fire made.

Everyone watched the door and filled themselves with Silence. In Silence all great magics are begun.

Then came the sound of beating wings. Great vast wings that each had known in their dreams.

Then Abraham stood up. He spoke quietly, but with an effect that showed he knew how to do magic with words.

"I put forth the Call, and the bold ones came sacrificing all to know all. Now their souls shine with dark light, and the forces of ignorance will know true fright. Ismeju comes, scenting them from afar, and the payment for life eternal is due."

The old ten rose up. Ingeborg gave Robert a kiss on the forehead. The ten walked to the door and beyond. Everyone gathered around to watch. The ten walked down the road toward the village.

The sound of wings, the sight of the black beyond black, the swiftness. It was like an owl snatching up a mouse. Ismeju grabbed up Ingeborg and her screams filled the night sky. Then it was done.

Robert closed his eyes for a moment.

He knew that he wanted one thing and one thing alone. It was a want that would change him utterly over the next three years. He would be the best. He had to be—to join her in Hell.

KISSING
SLEEPING BEAUTY

He got up an hour after sunset. The community college catalog lay in his mailbox and as always he was excited. Jacob was three hundred years old, which gave him at least two centuries on all the students and instructors, but his enthusiasm waxed greater than any ten of them. This after all was his life.

He paged through the catalog, savoring the feel of the fine-grained newsprint on his fingertips. After he had read the catalog once he would know it forever. He tossed the catalog into the gray plastic trash can and saw by his shadow that he had carelessly grown to his true height of eleven feet. He reached his long blue arm across the room to the light switch. Now it was Dark and he breathed in the darkness and began to *make*. He tried out the forms of the instructors from last semester. He adjusted each face in accordance with an internal mirror. Some of the forms felt very good, very natural as he fitted himself in them. These were the people whose philosophies—whose wide-ranging thoughts and memories—had assumed a cast very near his own. Of course he had taught two

of them. Dr. Gahdia had learned calculus and number theory from him in Benares thirty-five years ago. In those days sometimes Jacob became Raj Vajroli, internationally famous topologist, sometimes he became Zulfikkar Shukracharya, an Aghori who dwelt in the world's largest crematory grounds and taught the way of renunciation. Jacob had taught Marcel Fontenot, now an instructor in French, a scarce ten years ago, when Marcel took night classes at Tulane. Jacob had loved New Orleans and would have stayed there forever if the Dutchman hadn't spotted him drinking coffee at the Café du Monde at three in the morning during the most perfect thunderstorm.

The Dutchman would never track him here.

He hoped.

He walked over to the light switch and switched it on. Outside central air switched on and cool air played upon the beams of the "cathedral" ceiling. Three bedrooms. Two and a half baths. Three-quarter brick. Just like the house next door and the house next door and so on throughout the subdivision.

* * * * * * *

The family name had never been Van Helsing. That had been a pseudonym that great-great-grandpappy had given Bram Stoker, when great-great-grandpappy was stalking a vampire who was hiding in the London theatre district. He thought the young Irishman might be helpful. He hadn't counted on the book, being Dutch he hadn't realized that the Irish produce the

cream of English literature. Great-great-grandpappy had almost revealed too much—fortunately the movies confused things. The Dutchman braced himself for the jet's touchdown. He had never been good at air travel. He had flown into Stapledon once and his luggage had been lost. It had been scary explaining to airport officials that his suitcase contained three changes of clothes, a crossbow, and twenty surgical steel bolts.

"For hunting."

* * * * * * *

Sarah Gold lay on her brown plaid couch and thumbed through her Austin Community College catalog. Taking two night classes a semester had been a New Year's resolution four years ago and it had served her well. Of course, she hadn't had much use for Businessman's Arabic from last fall, but the important thing was the participation in the Myth of the Eternal Return. Her childless marriage prevented her from vicariously drawing off her children's autumnal protestations. Each year she was back in college. Young again and carefree. With each set of new people she peeled off some of the dull skin her passionless marriage had swathed her with. Robert wouldn't allow her to work. The classes—although they raised sinister uncertainties—seemed passive enough. You just soak up knowledge. Very feminine.

American History looked promising. Tuesday and Thursday nights. It might be a little left wing for Robert's tastes, but maybe she could sell it to him

in the guise of a renewed patriotism. She loved her country in away that Robert didn't. What she longed for most was the right to put a bumper sticker on her candy red Toyota Celica which read, "America, Love It and Improve It."

She reached down for her pen and the dryer alarm called.

* * * * * *

The downtown campus was cool because an underground stream ran beneath the buildings. Sweet gums, pecans, and ball moss-covered live oaks lined the streets. Jacob savored each footfall, each smell even the sour tang of buses, all the delectable shades of twilight chiaroscuro. Into the yellow light of the Old Main.

Jacob cleared his throat and Dr. Allen Rushton looked from his Xeroxed syllabuses—surprised to see a man looking exactly like Dr. Allen Rushton in the open doorway. The good doctor seemed even more surprised when he saw the stinger extend from Jacob's tongue.

Jacob blurred into him—savoring the snip of the stinger punching into the artery beneath the left ear. Dr. Allen Rushton began to dream of a tall blue man who spoke in a voice like unto the buzzing of bees. Something. Someone carried him home and tucked him in....

Jacob tossed the syllabuses in the trash. He began to type, "This course like most American history

surveys will begin with the invasion of the European peoples into lands held by the Amerindian peoples. We will begin by examining the intrusion of European sovereignty by means of conventional and biological warfare, and bait-and-switch modes of trade and diplomacy...."

* * * * * * *

The Dutchman checked into a Motel 6. He put his banner—the rune known as the thorn in brown on a beige background—on the eastern wall. He bowed toward Amsterdam, and then began to review his dossiers.

John Gahdia, BS, MS, PhD Mathematics, Benares University. b. 1931, began psychological treatment for attention disorder 1987. Fainting, dizzy spells. Anemia.

Eric Nordholdt, BA English Literature, University of Texas, MA French, Columbia. b. 1951 (remedial English, creative writing), 1989 resigned from ACC to pursue a career in visual arts after "having a series of fantastic dreams which leads me to a new understanding of Earth's history."

Peter LeFanu, BA, MA Philosophy, PhD Psychology, Duke University (Intro. Psych., Intro. Phil.) Two complaints have been lodged against Dr. LeFanu for teaching "bizarre and esoteric philosophical concepts relating to space, evolution, number, and geom-

etry." 1988. Dr.LeFanu dismissed such claims as "poppycock," stating that he is a confirmed materialist.

The Dutchman couldn't understand why a community college, but he didn't understand these types anyway. Maybe it was near a seat of power, perchance the vampire haunted the pink granite capitol building....

The Dutchman slapped his wrist. Never let yourself go. Never fantasize. If you go too far into the outer limits of consciousness they'll get you every time. That is where they truly lurk. He would need to get sufficient ID from his FBI connection. He'd long ago lost his accent. He could hunt anywhere.

* * * * * * *

Sarah Gold's heart thrilled. There was a dizziness, anew swooning—listening to Dr. Rushton. If she could just lay her head on the simulated wood desk she knew she'd fall into the most delicious sleep. Her eyelids were heavy but she managed to take notes into her orange spiral notebook. His eyes were so bright, his gestures and jokes appropriate. She was sure that all this material was being permanently etched into her brain. Everyone else leaned forward. Tranced out. Except for the freckled guy with the ginger hair. She wished he would stop squirming in his chair. Dr. Rushton just wasn't reaching him. She'd talked to him by the coke machine. He seemed—well, a little thick, but he was cute. Definitely very cute. Robert would beat her just for her thoughts. She squirmed in her chair too. But

that was for a different reason. She didn't know why this class created a generalized horniness. It might be the naughtiness. Sure, she supposed, white people coming to America was an invasion; but she'd never heard that word before. She'd never looked at history this way. The law of the forbidden.

Class was over. It took a moment or two for her to realize that everyone was leaving. That Dr. Rushton. She got up from her warm plastic seat and raced to the hall hoping to overtake Dr. Rushton. She caught him just before he was to open his broom-closet sized office. He flashed surprise, as though there were something inside he didn't want her to see. She knew that look. She'd always had a hard time talking to authority figures. She had to touch a brooch on her sweater before she could speak. Touch herself. Gold.

"Dr. Rushton, I know this is the first night, but could you give me some suggestions for the paper? What with volunteer work and teaching my Sunday school class and everything if I don't get started it'll never get done."

"Does anything spark your interest?"

"Well, I don't know a lot about American history. I mean, that's why I'm taking this course. For me, it's always been Columbus, Pilgrims, Tea Party, crossing the Delaware, the Civil War, we beat Germany twice, Korea, and then everything went sour. Not much of a history is it?"

"That you are looking, that people of your age and background are beginning to look at your history, is a

new historical force manifesting itself."

Goose pimples.

He continued, "If you can't think of a topic, some of my interests are: the draft riots of the Civil War—particularly the New York riots; the seizure of Cherokee lands by the state of Georgia; Frederick Douglass' editorials against the Mexican War; or Ignatius Donnelly and the People's Party."

"I don't know anything about those people."

"Not many do. I can be of some help. You have my office hours."

Sarah nodded.

"That's nice," he said. "Most people forget my office hours as soon as they write them down. I'm looking forward to working with you, Ms.—eh"

"Gold"

"Gold."

He walked down the hall and into the night. What was in the office? Why didn't he go in?

There was a man's voice behind her.

"I'd stay away from that creep."

She turned. The ginger-haired man stepped out from behind a column.

* * * * * * *

There are shadows even at night, and Jacob stepped into a shadow of a live oak and became one with its darkness. Most humans couldn't see him. He had smelled the predatory sweat. It might be the Dutchman, the current Dutchman. The woman was exciting. Her

mind was opening up to new ideas and he sensed, perhaps, the mating signal. He longed to lay another egg, create a beloved from the materials of himself. Waking sleeping beauty was always a dangerous business. He could try contacting the others. Some were in Berlin, Peking, Vilnius, Santo Andre. He could read the signs. He wanted—suddenly after decades of avoiding how own kind-- to reach out and touch them. But if the Dutchman was near he didn't dare. It was the woman. Sarah. She had brought him to life again. He was interested in furthering the kindred—a real desire again, not just the life maintenance tasks he'd been indulging in.

The noctiluca prevented him from seeing many stars, but he saw enough to make out the faces of the great old ones. Each though they were long finished with Earth—their will had formed patterns, geometrical representations of their pitiless love of mankind. In those days they didn't take human names. Conseen. Shelba. Lizleeth. Taur'n. Would he too evolve to move the stars? Of course, they didn't move the stars, but their impression caused anyone viewing the night sky to pick out the same patterns.

It was the woman.

He waited until the students had left, but before the janitors pushed their long T-brooms down the dusty corridors. He awakened Dr. Rushton mentally and saw that he made it safely to his car. He left him with a command to eat some beefsteak and spinach.

He took on the form of a man seen in the Dallas

airport one night. It had been an essence-exchanging glance, because he recognized something of himself in that other. The man had boarded a plane to Amarillo, and Jacob had never pursued the moment. Even for the immortal, there is only so much time. He boarded a Capitol Metro bus and rode home.

* * * * * * *

In his first two weeks of classes, the Dutchman had been able to put the mirror test to Drs. Gahdia and LeFanu. They weren't being used. If you see a face in the mirror that's different than the face you're aiming the mirror at-- then you've found one of them. It might be the American history prof or the archery instructor. Both had a rare intensity about them. That there had been one in this community was clear in the sharp eyes, voices, and attitudes. These things take years to cycle out. It would be better to bomb the city, but who knows how far the contagion might have spread? Some foreign student returned to Thailand, India, France? Some high school graduate who took criminology and now rides as a peace officer in the piney woods of Arkansas?

He lay back on the firm motel bed and stared at the red light of the smoke alarm. He wished he had some sensitivity to Them. That it all wasn't slow painful deductions—he could just walk down the streets— see that certain house with its sycamores and burst in. Knock down the white painted door and let loose with his crossbow. His predecessor had developed a feel for

them over the years—could spot them across Times Square on New Years Eve. But the sensitivity opened you up as well. Fight dragons long enough and you become a dragon. He'd heard that somewhere-- the men's room at Tokyo International Airport. He had had to put down his predecessor in Kansas City. He'd caught him talking to a group of adolescents about following your dreams. He shot him that night in the motel.

The red light.

* * * * * * *

Sarah Gold opened Joel Tyler Headley's *The Great Riots of New York, 1712 - 1873*. Robert had been none too happy when she had to get a book from Interlibrary Loan. Seemed to him, that if it was a good book about American history, our city library would have it. She had, of course, concealed the title from him. He was strictly against unrest. She read. She took notes. She began to see that Dr. Rushton was right. There was a connection between unrest and creativity. Liminal patterns of chaos. Society destroyed its own boundaries to permit new growth. He said that people were the same. Sometimes they had to remove their outer boundaries—in moments of love or fear or hate-- to grow in new ways. He said it was sad that society didn't understand the great riots as great outpourings of love—a desire from one element to create its beloved in the rest. He lectured on sex and love as political motivations—ways of "apprehending the good"—and

she knew that he was talking to her and her alone.

History was the way of making material things spiritual, and history had begun to open up for her. Everything she touched, everything she felt took on a sensuous quality. She could see so many secrets within. She would run her hand along the cool marble top of her grandmother's wash stand. She could feel the weariness of the hands washing the Depression-era dust from them. She could feel the heat of the East Texas porch and New deal dreams reflected off the dirty soap bubbles. When she picked up her ivory-handled soap brush she picked up her college days of the late sixties. Brushing her luxurious auburn hair before going to hear Allen Ginsberg "Om" into the microphone. How had she gone from that to this? How had she fallen asleep?

A history course wasn't supposed to restructure your life, was it?

And there was that sort of—well—glandular thing. Men had started to look good again. Even Robert, but Robert had left passion somewhere behind on the road to the perfect insurance agency. She'd been wanting to make contact with Dr. Rushton again, but he always disappeared after class. Going to his office seemed wrong. Too structured. Too student-teacher. She began hanging around with Eric, he was handsome and driven and above all mysterious. He never talked about where he was from, nor what he did, nor why he hated Dr. Rushton. Last night over coffee at Panchos, she let herself lean forward and ruffle his ginger hair.

She had no trouble reconciling her feelings for Eric and Dr. Rushton, and Eric's feelings toward Dr. Rushton. It all fit together somehow. Like a dream. Like it had been played through before.

* * * * * * *

There was only one class on the first floor Thursday night, and the Dutchman cut it. His hands shook a little as he picked the lock to Dr. Rushton's office; he could hear the distorted echo of the pseudo Dr. Rushton's voice from the classroom at the far end of the hall. The Dutchman's crossbow was in its black leather case, which lay on the golden terrazzo floor next to his sneakered feet. The lecture rose and fell, rose and fell. He probably had them all in trance by now—opening up their unconscious and planting all kinds of alien bits within. He could tell them just to sleep and step out in the hall. The Dutchman had cut only this one class, but that might be enough to tip his hand.

There. The tumblers turned and he grasped the slightly verdigrised brass knob with his gloved hands. As he had expected. The real Dr. Rushton slumped over his desk, a small pool of saliva collecting on its gray metal surface. The Dutchman pulled a very dim flashlight from his trouser pocket and pulled his gear inside, locking the door behind him.

He pulled out a small vial filled with an oily brown liquid.

* * * * * * *

Jacob had just reached his summation on Nat Turner when he felt Dr. Rushton awake. He tried to send a mental command to sleep, but someone was applying a painful stimulus: iodine to the bite mark. So the Dutchman had found him. Probably that creepy guy that never achieved trance. Jacob had been too drawn to Sarah. She had gone so far—he had poured so much of his mind into her, that he desired her utterly. If only she awakened this night, he would've begat a beloved to spend the dark centuries with. He mustn't run. He had to think and move in his own time. It was the only means of survival. He could put Sarah in the crises that would awaken her—or kill her. He must do it. Love without pity. If you ever pitied them, you were lost. The stake or worse. If you had compassion rather than pitiless love, they would turn on you like the animals they were. Sarah opened her congenital blue eyes, and stared at him. Sometimes humans surfaced from trance just be patient with them and they would return. When Carla had trained him she told him that. She begat him when he was a divinity school student in Hamburg. A short hundred years later she passed into the next stage of Being. Sarah closed her eyes and returned to trance. He finished his lecture.

"Ms. Gold, could I speak to you after class?"

* * * * * * *

Her heart was in her throat. She'd managed to send him the mating signal. She didn't know how she had done it. Maybe it was automatic. She'd been thinking

and reviewing—assembling the materials of her life—and she was ready. Ready to go anywhere with him. If he said Mexico she would drive to Mexico and Robert would have faded from her mind in a hundred miles. How she knew this was love when she hadn't kissed him or spoke to him or touched him, she did not know. But that he opened so much in her was a sign of love. He'd put a riot in her soul by stirring up the fires of the past against the banal ice of the present. She'd been trying to do that to herself for years, with class after class. And isn't that love, when the other empowers you to fulfill your own dreams? That meant that she was leaving history and entering a new realm. She remembered that Kissinger quote he'd written on the blackboard. "The iron law of history is that no desire is ever completely fulfilled." If she went beyond history, she became something beyond human.

All of this was in a flash as if the air suddenly grew clear around her. The other students—middle-aged collegians like herself, working kids, hangers on—filed out. Car doors slammed and wheels-on-gravel noise followed. She was alone with Dr. Rushton.

"Sarah, could you give me a lift tonight? My car is in the shop."

"Sure, Dr. Rushton."

"Allen."

"Allen."

His words seemed so conventional, as though this was an average pick-up—or strictly speaking what TV and romances had instructed her to believe an

average pick-up was. She couldn't remember how it was with Robert, the one part of her story that refused to awaken, perhaps because she was finished with it. But had she misjudged this man? Should she take her growing awareness and run?

He turned off the fluorescent lights and they walked out of the classroom.

She asked, "Don't you need to go by your office or something?"

"No. The main function of an academic office is as a place to steal pens and paperclips from."

Down the terrazzo floored hall and out the main door into the warm cedar-scented night of the porch. Past the great arched columns across the soft grass and onto the asphalt of the parking lot where her Toyota was parked (its candy red stolen by the night). And as they approached the car someone stood up on the other side of the car and pointed a...a crossbow? at them.

"Release the woman. Your time is up," said Eric.

"What a terrible way to express jealousy," she said.

Dr. Rushton had become very calm and elegant in gesture. He said, "You're very young, new at this I'd guess. I suppose with the great value your family places on human life, I would be safe if I held her in front of me as shield."

Eric said, "I would kill you both. She is probably unfit for human society now."

Dr. Rushton smiled, "You people are getting much more cold-blooded. Sarah, I suggest that you circle around the car and stand with our Dutch friend. When

he fires his bolt, you should make a run for it. Those cedars might form a good shield."

Sarah said, "What's going on here? I'm going to get the police."

Eric said, "The police will back me up. The police have always had a healthy suspicion of new ideas. If you'll walk away from the vampire voluntarily, I'll let you live. It's probably the wrong thing to do, but we strive for humanity first."

She turned to Dr. Rushton. His eyes seemed as stars. He gently shook his head no. He said, "Sarah, there is no reason for this stupid one to kill you. Please, dear one, walk over to him."

"He called you a vampire."

"He's correct. I live off human beings. As people think my thoughts, they energize me. If enough of them have taken my way of being into themselves, I'll survive even if he fires that bolt. Sadly I don't think I've succeeded I've only been at this since 1690. You've seen the pattern in class. Sometimes a great notion takes hold of a group of people—they run with it awhile and then they drop it. That marks one of our failures. Sometimes it continues like the American Revolution. One of our successes."

"Move, lady, or I'll have to shoot you too."

"Please, Sarah, join him."

"But why don't you turn into a bat or something and flyaway?"

"I'm afraid I'm limited to humanoid forms. My race looked a great deal like yours, when the nova flare

destroyed our world. My adopted race, I began human like you."

Sarah walked around the car toward Eric. All of this was happening too fast. She had to wake up from this nightmare. Eric squeezed off a shot. The bolt thudded into Dr. Rushton's chest and the air smelled of bad eggs. Dr. Rushton didn't fall, he faded. She could see through him—see his ruptured multi-chambered heart—his eyes had fixed, the pupils large as dimes. A dark-colored saliva had begun to drip from his mouth. Eric was rapidly cranking up the crossbow—slipping another bolt in place. She fumbled through her black vinyl purse. She had to stop this. There. She grabbed the little cylinder of mace that Robert made her carry. She sprayed it full into Eric's face. He bent double and began to puke, firing his bolt into the front tire of her Toyota. Dr. Rushton solidified a little. She could still see the doorway of the college through him. He pulled the bolt from his chest. It made a sucking sound.

"Why aren't you dead?"

"Because of you, Sarah. You're maintaining me with your mind. That's the risk the vampire race took when they came here. After a long wearying swim through space, they found a stupid primate and they hoped that the primate would like to grow, think, evolve. They poured the whole of themselves into the primates— making what you would call the preconscious. For millennia they lived there in dreams, their presence stirring up creativity and dreams in what came to be mankind. But there were exceptions. People in

whom we could not dwell—bloodlines of stupidity, that fought against us like antibodies fight against an infection. They tracked down reformers, thinkers, men of vision. So we stepped out of the darkness of your unconscious minds and became as we once were. We fight to waken humanity—a creative race that can survive—carryon the essence of change and evolution—for as long as those ideas persist, we persist. The Dutchman there fights for the right of humanity to sleep. No more worries, pain, frustration. Just monkey happiness. Their weapons are darts and thorns."

"And me? What's there for me?"

"Sometimes a human awakes and joins us. We give them tools to become as we. They get the limitations too. They remember the nova flares and can't withstand the light of day. I was human once, but I was transformed—there being much from outside to work upon. We begat only adult children—the opening of minds is our means of reproduction. So tell me Sarah, what is there for you?"

She looked at the puking Dutchman and then considered the prospect of waking minds a thousand years from now. She walked over to Jacob and took his cold hand. And they walked into a mist, which seemed to come from nowhere. And soon there was only night and the Dutchman.

POE, ON THE
MORNING AFTER

After the visits of my vampire lover
After the bites and the bruises
From my harsh cruel muses
After the 1000th time of wondering if she *really* is a
  vampire
My world becomes a shaky nauseating kaleidoscope
Now fever dream, now chilly weakness
Now summer, now winter.
Now flowers, now ash.
Ah, I remember it was in the bleak of December
And I, a dying ember, wrought my ghost upon the
  floor
And as I fade into that final ashy dream I tell myself
The remedy for my pain
Is the pain itself.

ABOUT THE AUTHOR

DON WEBB has had sixteen books published, and some of his material has been translated into eleven languages. He fell in love with Science Fiction in grade school, and had his first professional stories published in 1983 in *Interzone*. He is equally attracted to the pre-Golden Era science fiction as he is to the experiments of the New Wave, and tries to synthesize both in his writing. He teaches high school English as well as classes for UCLA extension.

As a Texan, he has a secret chili recipe, enjoys his home in Austin, and has been a fixture for many years at the local SF convention, Armadillocon. He grew up in the days of the 'zine revolution, and has a love for the small press, as well as places that occasionally send him cash. He lives with his lovely wife Guiniviere and two cats. He is not as funny as he thinks he is.

You can reach him at:

writebydonwebb@gmail.com